Sempiternal Solo

Liminal Books is an imprint of Between the Lines Publishing. The Liminal Books name and logo are trademarks of Between the Lines Publishing.

Cover Artwork: Kamilla Sims

Cover Design: Morgan Bliadd

Between the Lines Publishing
1769 Lexington Ave N, Ste 286
Roseville MN 55113
btwnthelines.com

First Published: November 2024

ISBN: Paperback 978-1-958901-95-3

ISBN: Ebook 978-1-958901-96-0

Library of Congress Control Number: 2024942217

Sempiternal Solo

Joseph Gibson

For Oliver

Lunar Dance

"Some realms constitute the arts as the main focus for their society."

- Yonet; a Typhame cartographer

Lola stood still, an early night's whisper touching her hair like a friend and rippling her sundress like magic, the hair as dark as crow feathers, the sundress royal blue. Smooth rolling hills elevated her a bit closer towards the moon's embrace, and the grass around her swayed effortlessly, waiting patiently. The calm, cool scenery welcomed those visiting to observe the stars floating beyond the atmosphere. Lola knew this place was more than a simple venue, however, but a stage, one set to come alive with motion.

Her feet remained firm on the ground, her heart thumping as she watched the surrounding fireflies and glowtail swallows rise from their homes amid the grass blades. They took notice of the lady standing atop the hill face and, to a more profound extent, the violin cradled in her hands. She held it like one might a newborn child, and for a moment everything felt like a dream set upon a moonlit stratum, an ethereal plane where all seemed magnificent, flowing, drenched with nostalgia. But these nights were common during the warm months of Strevenfall, a realm where enchantment like this could thrive and prosper.

The fireflies continued watching as Lola raised her instrument and bow, setting them into a fine balanced posture, a grand overture held within the form of her limbs. Her feet parted slightly, displacing their weight as to hold perfect balance, ready to spin and whirl about once the notes sped up. She laid her bow across the four silver threads and recalled her previous practice rounds on this same hill, over and over, pondering each step until they merged like a subconscious reel playing back in her mind. These snapshots of the past ran between her thoughts, movements learned by rote, sequences written throughout her brain.

Be still.

Breathe.

It was time to play.

Lola began. Her bow slid along the wires for a high note wavering free about the air, her eyes closed, her head bowed against the chinrest. She flew carefully around the upper octaves of sounds as she wove them together, then down a little, then up, her mouth stretching in satisfaction, playing the next adagio as if it were a language spoken by an expert, as if music was a puzzle easily solved. These were good melodies to start, fine for a short stay, but that was all. Now the bow angled and quickened to produce a snappy plethora of mid keys, and she moved with the tempo, her dress moving in long swells of silk. Louder she went, gradually, cautiously, giving each new sound space to breathe before the next one resonated, at times picking off the ends of notes to make a few staccatos. She breached higher volume and held it flawlessly, the decibel clean and rich. There was a world to explore here, this myriad of notes ranging from flat to sharp. The tones embellished their shapes, some retaining their separation while others spoke with smooth transitions. Her pace jolted slightly, turning the previously slow tempo into one of agile harmonies. Wind blew as if approving this new changed rhythm, cool and smooth and flowing past her clothes, her hair.

A stabbing cold twinged her body. It was ignored.

Lola breathed, stopping to rest and regard the smooth greenery of hills watched by stars. Another breeze slid across the grass, a welcome presence that quivered the ocean of her dress, rippling the fabric, maybe brushing off some dust. A far-off crowd might have mistaken her for a midnight wisp, a figure draped in blue. Her cobalt eyes narrowed as the reel continued in her mind, the next step, the next sound, the future image of her dancing about with every second staged seamlessly, without friction between one move and the next. It was a blur that would grow more hazed the longer she rested. Movement was the only state of being able to catch up, to flourish.

Her focus clung to the strings as she raised her violin again. One step at a time. First, picture the path, then walk its face.

Another stabbing cold struck her, also ignored.

The performance resumed. The octaves combined as she granted her bow freedom to slant at its leisure, giving leeway into new formations more complex than before, new chords with altered progressions. She could hop between these levels, pitching her tones, growing louder, more distinct, maturing its density. The fireflies lifted in unison as they watched Lola stray from her spot and move about. Her feet glided across the grass as if she were in the arms of an invisible partner—dancing slowly, making sure not to step on her toes, or trip—a waltz conscious of every sound. She let loose a trill of characters sewn together with smooth legato intervals, climbing up the scale then wrapping around with more intricate patterns. And just when it seemed like the phase would end, she jumped off the ledger line and performed a high presto of short, brisk accents to tie up the chord with emphasis. The flies and swallows stirred as if reacting to a mystic force. She snapped into focus every detail no matter how much her fingers cramped in protest. Everything streamed along, and though not entirely synchronized with the mental image of her, she didn't plan on stopping, not yet. She whirled about. There were no clear spaces between her movements as she played faster, giving her instrument torture with heightened tempo.

Another stab.

Cold.

Crippling.

And this time a knotted pain curled in her stomach, and she flinched, the next sound stifled, mutated. Her bow hand stiffened as her fingers locked, the last note leaving her strings as a choking whine, like a static discharge. Her body doubled over as the bow dropped to the ground with a soft thud, and suddenly her instrument felt so cold it burned. She stumbled, lurched, the fireflies falling back to earth leaving tiny glimmers speckled on the grass. Gradually, she knelt, letting the pain drone by, waiting for the sharp tingling of her eardrums to fade. Like an old friend, it brought a sad familiarity, seeing that phantom image continue playing away with harmful intent, dancing gingerly until it vanished with a smug wink, but there was nothing to be done now, for the session had died. One misstep would leave a crowd disappointed even if all else was played perfectly. They would be dismayed, angry, and laughing.

"By the stars," she muttered, "another wasted play."

After a lengthened pause and a mental curse, Lola rose, feeling her dress heavier—a cloak of ice as it slumped down upon her shoulders. Faceless attendees laughed behind tight lips in her mind, even though no one watched in reality. Once refreshing passes of wind now seemed to creep over her, prickling her skin. It was best if she returned home and revise her mistakes—again—much like the weeks before.

Indeed, another night wasted.

It was a long way back home. She strolled along the lone narrow sidewalk winding towards her small subdivision, passing an Aezial sanctuary made of domed marble with enormous pillars, around which the expansive grass meadows were broken only by pale stone gazebos. Even those of prestigious taste would have at least stopped to admire parts of it, but Lola's half-closed stare never strayed from the ribbon of concrete sliding beneath her feet. That is, until she glanced up to get bearings on the moon's position and sighed. It was well past midnight, well into the morning hours. Time had fallen by faster than expected, and it made her finally notice a certain weight crowned on her eyelids, how tired she was, how weak she felt. It was understandable, absolutely. Playing for hours on end had made her seem brittle-like, her arms set to drop the violin she carried. Perhaps if she walked with more assertion, a few bones might snap. Then, there she would stay, a mound of ice crystals on the smooth, ivory path. Nature's sounds neglected to break the silence here, so her mind often wandered into thinking such metaphors, even if some were simply ridiculous.

It was when the first few streetlamps rose into view that Lola knew she was close, their tawny gold halos making her shadow visible once she passed under them. Her body flickered on and off with each lamp saying a quick hello before turning her dark again.

She rounded a corner leading to a wider road.

Large, blackened bodies of apartment complexes looked down from either side, with the scent of musky bricks wafting up her nose, the standard for humid weather. They were nice residences nonetheless, each structure bound to the next by complex fretwork designs, with picket fences and well-trimmed gardens encircling her own apartment, which was located in the fourth building down from where the street began. Her space was on the second floor, where it had been waiting for hours.

Up the stairs, turn a corner, walk several feet, and stop. Lola pulled a small nickel key from one of her flats. She leaned against the heavy door, because pushing it open would have sapped away her last remaining energy. After the latch closed softly, her limbs loosened, and she let free a listless breath of air. A bedroom, kitchen, bathroom, and a living room formed an even square within these walls, a rather small living space, but there was no other place like it at the price. She set the violin and bow back in their case, the one that, admittedly, had been purposely left behind. Lola seldom carried it unless she was making a trip into the city, which had recently been more of a rare occurrence with most classes already over for the year.

5

After brushing away a few strands of hair, she bathed, changed, ate dinner, and did so with such weariness that the memory of her wasted night only came back as she swung into bed, just before letting that familiar, drowsy weight finally run its course.

Across the bedroom were snow-colored squares, a stand holding an open booklet of sheet music. The window nearby doused pale rays across the paper.

"Please, not now," Lola whispered. It was crazy talking to an object, but she nevertheless wanted a look at it. The bed complained as its passenger rose off, and she nearly stumbled towards the booklet of sounds stored within blanch parchment. "Hummingbird's Verse" was scripted in large cursive font near the top, and below, a sea of symbols contained within their rails peered back at her, a plethora of signs in all shapes and sizes. This song was flying off her strings not an hour ago, eight and a half pages of dynamic chords connected with slur lines, rests, repeats, and all manner of markings constructing the extensive piece. She'd once heard that no one could ever sing "Hummingbird's Verse" completely, not a human, merfolk, elf, or anyone, suggesting that only an instrument played by hand could explore this music in its entirety. It was also why she believed the lyrics were discarded a long time ago and the song was orchestrated into a purely wordless creation. She only remembered vaguely seeing a version of the song with spoken words strung below its notes, an early memory so far back in time that she'd forgotten how it came to be.

She turned the first page, fingers touching along the snow, exposing another layer of sounds trapped in parchment, passing a line where the tempo and pitch climaxed, bringing forth a crescendo, one of the more emotional parts. Past that was a short rest, then a set of eighth notes played in glissando, meaning to slide between them. All of it was rather easy compared to other sections or even other works of music at this difficulty level, though it still appeared like a forest of ink. However, she knew harder portions waited underneath a few more layers.

Page four came along, a jumbled mayhem of keys and symbols latticed together. And here it was, the measure where one had to jump around the sharp scale with a tremolo, performed by rapidly moving the bow back and forth against a string to create a wavering effect that produced slightly different pitches than normal, prominent overtones. This spot was where her mind had faltered. It was why she'd stumbled on the hillside. It was why she'd stumbled so many nights before. Even after weeks of meticulous rehearsal, this incomprehensible maze still appeared as it was, a maze, and every time a journey was made through it, she never failed to ruin things. Time had stubbornly refused to let her solve the issue even with long spans of practice. Nothing clicked. Sure enough, and with bitter disappointment, it looked as though her ability wouldn't suffice on its own.

They would be dismayed, angry, and laughing.

"I need help," Lola whispered to the moon, and its glow replied mutely, like a guardian whose presence alone spoke volumes.

She did, after all, attend one of Strevenfall's most esteemed universities, known for specializing in the advanced musical domain, and that said plenty coming from a realm where the arts already had a firm hold on society. It would be best to visit her teacher there and share dialogue of her dilemma, and luckily, this teacher was someone to whom she already had close companionship with—Mr. Krayble. He was a wise soul who taught many, only to befriend a few. Krayble normally welcomed those who wanted tutoring regardless of the hour. She would pay him a visit come sunrise.

House of the Arctic Circle

"An arena at Garenham can hold exactly 2,500 people, not including the glass sky decks."

- An advertisement from Faben's newspaper

Sandy's Diner was a small outlet for those wanting a short meal, oftentimes of club sandwiches and pasta glorified to drastic measures with toppings of all kinds. Lola's morning shift saw many customers, but she hardly noticed them from the kerosene stoves and choppers around back. A thin veil of grease always managed to coat her face by rotation's end, and while the work was in some ways liberating, its passing brought more relief than anything else. The manager, Iris, had on several occasions offered her a spot up front, taking orders.

"People enjoy a pretty face when they walk in," Iris would say, smiling. "Perhaps you'll even find a lover."

Each offer was simply declined. Going about performing rote greetings and follow-ups had never looked appealing.

Lola washed her face, then discarded the apron and rags for a plain olive skirt and top, her violin case slung around the shoulder. It was just heavy enough so that its presence couldn't be ignored, but thankfully she never had to carry it long. Chatter rang from the passersby as she walked to the nearest street curb and waved for transport. Horse-drawn carriages traveled down the roads, winding through town, some holding bodies with lavish suits and faces peppered with perfume, while some wore traditional clothes, or even simpler attire like hers. Most carriages here were owned publicly. Some were rented. A vacant one met her on the curb, hooves clacking the pavement.

The driver looked down. "Where to young lady?"

"Garenham's north university campus, 557 Drave Street." Lola was set to hand out proper change when a flock of snow sparrows fluttered overhead, their numbers massive. Sunlight flitted past their wings, casting shadows that raced on the ground below. Everyone stopped to look on as children went about attempting to catch the shadows, stomping playfully, laughing.

Lola gave it all only a second's glance before continuing inside the carriage. It was an unsteady drive to the campus. The carriage rattled to every malformation the road offered, and the boisterous chatter from outside had no intention of dying. Even so, she often picked out handfuls of sound from the ruckus and made internal beats from it, not exactly caring about what sounds stitched together. This was merely a good exercise to further develop her sense of rhythm. Only their importance at face value mattered in creating melodies, even if it was still a mess to think about.

Momentum from the ride's stop pulled her forwards, a rude reminder that there was still a transport fee to pay. She slung the case back over her shoulder and pushed the door flap open, letting a breeze sift through her hair and face. She stepped out with a few coins and a simple thanks, as if that was payment enough.

Garenham's campus was a large, spired complex with sculptures and fountains ringed by sidewalks of clean white pavement. Many described these grounds as representing a great Aezial palace gifted with grand sheets of stained glass. Brilliant beams of light gleamed down the huge panes with colors so rich they could have devoured the comparably minuscule lady walking under them. A freshman was almost guaranteed to get lost on their first day, or week, but Lola was four months away from becoming a senior now and knew that Mr. Krayble's seminar was far west of the main office.

Students grouped together in small clusters along the halls, their noises such that Lola could again make inner songs and beats. Even if class hours had come and gone, some still visited these squares to talk about common artful tastes. Even those who did not attend Garenham came to visit the statues and other monuments of intricate design, like the grand clockwork tellurion, its size larger than a small house, displaying a model of Strevenfall and other realms slowly orbiting Aezial with meticulous accuracy. Lola passed it without pause or even the pretense of attention. She walked steadily about the halls, making turns, taking no heed of the paintings and sculptures sliding to and from her sight.

The tall wooden doors of the auditorium were nearly impossible to open if one didn't use both hands. They creaked and vibrated as she heaved on them, like a whale's call rumbling through the hinges.

Massive. It was a lecture with shafts of sunlight filtered through a ceiling composed mostly of multicolored glass. Rows and rows of seats and stands funneled down a slight incline towards the wooden stage dais elevated at the center. If music had its favorite sanctuaries, this would be one of them. Lola made the long journey down the aisle, each step muffled by dark blue carpeting. A few students were scattered about this indoor landscape, some erect before their stands with instruments, others settled in chairs reading or committing time towards schoolwork. A few turned at her presence before resuming their activities, but she was searching for one face in particular.

Someone tall with a purple suit and tie stood near a group of freshmen at the bottom row. Like most of Strevenfall's population, her music instructor was elven with slightly pointed ears, though his own drooped with age. Being human, Lola wondered how it might feel to have ears like those, but the notion perished as she neared him. She pulled back her shoulders to at least appear more professional regardless of her offhand apparel. It was too casual for such a meeting.

Should've brought finer clothes.

Krayble's attention shifted to her before she could tap his shoulder. "Miss Pern! At last, someone who actually knows practice makes perfect, and that it yields better results than cramming." He partially turned to the group behind and added, "A prime example of one who completes her assignments on time."

A boy from the group raised a scribbled paper. "Ninety-nine percent done is done to me!"

Lola tried chuckling along with the others, but the word 'perfect' pinched her mind, like a warning bite that faded moments later, for Krayble's undivided attention was on her now, a silent prompt for her to speak first.

"Making new friends?" she asked.

The elf's nose scrunched as he shrugged. "Perhaps, if they weren't fond of late work, five hours late to be exact. Head of staff urged me to go easier on the freshmen this year."

"Classes always lighten up when exams draw near. Reviewing a year's worth of material takes time."

"Oh, just another common excuse for them to prioritize mage classes, I say." He waved airily. "We may be a school centered around the arts, but unfortunately, the basics always get shoved in at the end, and classes like mine become more of an afterthought."

Lola wasn't sure how the topics related, but she didn't want to waste time discussing the matter now.

"But I'm being dramatic," he added with haste. "Now before you accuse me of complaining, how about telling me what brings you here outside your normal class schedule?"

They both grinned because she'd raised a finger to do just that. "It's a first for me, I know. Well, there's a certain piece that's been giving me a hard time lately. I've some theories why, but they're just theories. Maybe it's one part, or a harmony I'm not grasping. It definitely calls for extra help with someone who knows better."

"Something with music giving *you* trouble? Nonsense." Krayble mused a bit. "What's the name?"

"'Hummingbird's Verse'," she replied, adjusting her case strap, "a song meant to be played on string and bow, but it can be done on different instruments all the same."

They walked the short trio of steps leading up to the dais stage, a platform with mostly blue rays coming down in droves, coating the stage with arctic lambency. Some doused a piano nearby, a few scattered stands surrounding it, along with short rolling benches.

"Do excuse the mess. Remnants of last evening's concert still remain."

"It's quite alright. I'm just sorry for not being there to hear it."

"Was it because you were indulging in late-night practice again?"

"Of sorts, yes." Lola gave the elf a copy of "Hummingbird's Verse" as they sat opposite. Krayble looked it over, or rather, he analyzed it. Decades of masterful experience poured across the paper. His eyes were that of spotlights searching through the crevices of notes in a way that surpassed her understanding. She frequently admired the act. This man could turn on these spotlights whenever necessary, a predisposed instinct, and turn them off acting like he'd merely skimmed the surface.

"It's not a children's nursery rhyme, that's for certain." He brought over a stand to lean the pages on. "I'd put this song at near mastery level in terms of complexity—not something I would ever teach here. This is the likes of which an orchestra might play at The Grand Hall, or maybe for a top-tier competition."

Lola set her violin into playing position. "I take it you want me to start fresh from the beginning?"

"Now Miss Pern, don't imply that our normal class routine has escaped you."

She offered a smirk, as if hearing an old joke. "Of course not. Warm up always comes first."

The arena's architecture was made for sound to bounce off the wooden floor and spread evenly throughout. Lola's practice scales resonated across the massive room, freed of obstacles that would normally cause them to echo; a world without detainment or suppression. Her notes touched the ears of students scattered across the rows of seats, diverting their attention down to where she sat with straightened posture and what some might've described as near-flawless style.

They were watching.

Watching her shoulders.

Her hands.

Her movements.

Lola felt each pair of eyes roll down her back like cold beads of water, or perhaps it was sweat brought on by nervousness. Either way, this feeling grew as she played on steadily, going up the scales, back down, then up, much like her breathing—inhale, exhale, one at a time. Playing alone before a crowd was an undertaking she'd normally avoid, and among the reasons why she practiced on the rolling hills outside of town, where nobody would ever find her, and upon further realization, another reason why she'd never asked for additional tutoring with Krayble beyond regular class sessions. He would send each student to this same spot and perform in front of an unsuspecting audience. To him, the extra attention was a good thing, apparently.

Thankfully, she finished the last scale without issues.

"Very nice. Now onto some real material, shall we?" Krayble scooted behind Lola's seat so as to follow along with "Hummingbird's Verse".

It was a guilty pleasure having this song already edged deep within memory. Lola could plummet the world into darkness by closing her eyes, and hopefully forget about those watching beyond the blackness. With steady hands, her bow began its long journey through the first few lines of music, making sure each note performed to their utmost quality. When put on a stage filled with spotlights, playing perfectly was a must. A skipped rest would ultimately end up like a disastrous fallout with no way of warming up again, embarrassing to every doll who watched.

Dolls? she thought. *I'm...thinking of dolls?*

The arduous trek continued on through the first climax as she whisked off a smoothly strung plethora of keys rising with pitch. For one split second, a chilled crack of light rippled through her enclosed vision, which nearly made her stumble, a detriment given that this was a relatively easy part of the song. If she faltered now, a doll would be added to the bunch.

Ridiculous. Stop thinking about dolls, idiot.

Now came the section where her path twisted, full of notes skipping around on opposite spectrums, and of course, that tremolo, which climbed up its tangled progression at near-incomprehensible speed. She had to breathe right when the climb began, then let it out, not too fast, not too slow. Either mistake would be very apparent even to those who'd never listened to "Hummingbird's Verse" prior. Krayble's stare was fixed like a pulled wire about to snap. He was ready to detect any small error despite his calm, almost vacant expression.

Steady, she thought. *Shoulders set. Back arched.*

But they were watching.

Cold water down her back.

A frigid pain tugged at her chest, choking her next breath, but thankfully she managed the rigorous stanza free of errors. For a moment she thought to revisit the bright world of people and regard whatever had caused the pain, but the idea fell away, for there was no time to catch figments of imagination. More intricate parts lingered ahead, waiting to be played off and judged among faces with silk for skin, and threaded stitches for mouths.

Dolls again? Stop it!

Inhale, exhale, one at a time, over and over. It wasn't hard to breathe, right? Lola was a decent way through the piece now, progressing through the section where a once smooth connected style suddenly merged into one full of tightened notes, sounding just off tune enough so that listeners

14

caught the eeriness of it; a haunted chord. This was the part of "Hummingbird's Verse" that one played with a more devilish texture, as if she was beating the violin to submission, not caring for its plea or heeding its retorts.

The cold tugged again, harder. Her eyes snapped open in pain as it swelled somewhere within. A bead of sweat slithered down her chin, falling below—a slight drop. Another tug followed, harder still, like a frozen glitch up her spine. More seconds ticked away, each one tied with heavy silence, making her ears ring, making her body jolt as if she'd been rammed with ice.

"Trouble, Miss Pern?"

Krayble's question hung, too long.

"Your last phrase came out ragged. Remember not to play those sixteenth notes as accidental staccatos."

Lola stiffened. She hurriedly wiped sweat off her brow. "L-let me start a line before, from the last rest."

The elf verged on coming closer, teetering between standing and staying, but decided on the latter. "Sure thing. Whenever you're ready."

It was more difficult to resume where the tempo had already quickened. Even so, this felt less daunting than starting fresh, and truthfully, she thought retracing prior sections would bring another cold flash of pain, and more images bearing faceless bodies of sewn flesh. She tried achingly to keep her instrument angled right, but gravity felt strangely powerful, its pull growing every time a note left her strings. Another flash splintered. Another image. There was no stopping this, that much was for certain. It was certain the cold wasn't imaginary, nor the pain causing her to pause every other line now. More dolls flooded into her brain with aimless stares, like being diagnosed with a terminal illness.

Please...stop.

A glacier crawled up her feet, her calves, thighs, chest, and her face, feeling numb there. For a moment she considered what might happen if

15

another key was missed, another mistake. The cold would increase, over and over. The pain would swell, again and again.

Another flash, this time intolerable.

And the song fell apart. Lola's bow died and threatened to slip from her hands, a quavering shriek vibrating across the arena as its last note died. Her body locked, and she found herself shaking, bones, fingers, feet, head throbbing. Krayble was saying something, but it was muffled to an echo bouncing off her mind.

A hand found the lady's shoulder; a stroke though the haze.

"This is a difficult piece," Krayble said once more. "I can tell you're letting nervousness have its way. Now, you know what to do. Take a second, step back, and see what went wrong—"

"It's easier on the piano, perhaps," Lola cut him off, wiping her face again.

"This isn't like you. What's wrong?"

But she'd already placed the violin back in its coffin, balling her hands into pale fists to keep from shaking. "Nothing's wrong. I'm taking a step back as you suggested. Let's just use the piano, alright?"

"Well, if you want to…" Krayble looked at her as if regarding someone different, a student whose complexion had changed. If he were to touch her again, she might have cracked so loud his ears would shatter.

"Here, see?" Lola's hand shivered near the paper, pointing at a section where notes twined together in complex knots and loops. "These are simpler to play using this sort of instrument." She seated the piano bench. By now, everyone watched with raw attention, their spotlights beaming chilled light upon her, making her pores brittle, the space frozen, filled with faceless bodies.

Dolls.

Krayble, without releasing his stare from her, gestured to those who looked on and said, "All of you get back to work!"

Mostly everyone complied, although mumbling among themselves. Their whispers were static in Lola's brain. It was humiliating to fail repeatedly under the judgment of others. Hence why Krayble's stare alone made her wish their meeting would end.

"Starting from the same rest again, Miss Pern?"

"Y-yes sir."

"Fine, whenever you're ready." The elf crossed his arms. "But Lola, I'm not blind, and I'm getting worried. I recommend you tell me what's really going on after this. Understand?"

Krayble hardly ever addressed students by their first name. His doing so now meant he was, in fact, worried.

Lola nodded, spreading her fingers a hair's width above the keys.

Inhale. Exhale. One at a time.

She relied on muscle memory to conduct herself, wanting nothing more than to leave on good terms. Closing her eyes would only manifest the same nerve-chilling images again. There was nowhere to go. The only way to exist was out here. She tried everything to ignore the vise straining her bones, and not to break in front of everyone. Her eyes raced across the paper; her pulse heightened to where she felt it run beneath her wrists.

Then, one final image wormed through Lola's mind, and her body froze, her vision blurred around the edges. The piano keys were cold bars of iron and she jerked away, panting. The arena stirred with everyone muttering louder, too loud, exchanging confused glances as if to pass around a contagious, unknown disease.

Apparently, she'd screamed too, for Krayble was sitting on the bench next to her in efforts to make eye contact. His mouth was moving but no sound came. Everything was mute, a silent ring.

"Miss Pern, can you hear me!" Krayble touched her back and she rose instantly, like she'd been hauled up with puppet strings.

"Miss Pern," he whispered. "What's gotten into you?"

Lola backed away, slowly, a hand clasped over her mouth, horrified, trembling. She looked as though someone had been maimed right before her eyes.

"What's going on? Say something!" Krayble stepped closer.

But Lola didn't reply. In one hectic motion she scooped up the coffin and whatever dignity she had left. Everybody watched her storm out the arena, all wearing vacant, concerned, or even frightened faces. Their eyes penetrated beneath her skin, leaving a sense of curglaff deep within her chest.

Bring Me Hoarfrost

"A syncing moment keeps us home, the winter outside, and the combines of rooms tangled with time. Blizzards howl as we stay up in bed. Snowfall sings about present days falling when the clocks change their tune. The seasons pause to soften our minds, until we rest, warm yet cool under the covers. A sea of dreams drowns out the noise, the voices, the nature beyond. Then we start to wonder, sleepwalking underwater, if it all makes sense to others. Silver linings shatter on a world far from here, but the crashing of waves is all we can hear. Little one, tell them your body is a notion, that you're ready to see the world before it fades out of view. It starts with a breath, a moment of cold as frost collects on the sill. Let's feed our thoughts to a hiemal life, burning less through midnight's embrace..."

- "Hummingbird's Verse"; lyrics part 1

The apartment door opened and closed silently as Lola stepped in. She entered as if coming from a blizzard outside, relieved to finally be separated from the world, away from dolls and spotlights everywhere. Yet her hand remained on the doorknob, squeezing it until her fingers turned pale. She let go, eventually, backing slowly towards the living room, heart racing, then slowing down more... more, letting off its high.

She sat tiredly before the kitchen counter, head in hands, hands shaking even with her pulse steadied to manageable proportions. Her violin slept in its coffin nearby, but she still felt as if the instrument watched her.

Lola moved, expecting the dim, early afternoon glow to quell her mood, only to find its light harsh and crass across her face. With a weighted sigh she pushed dolefulness away and indulged a little in some homemade pleasures. Perhaps putting more food in her system, changing clothes, and washing her hair would make things less of a dumb, depressed remnant of what had transpired.

After washing up, her hair cleaned, the shaking had reduced tenfold. Wearing pajamas, Lola flipped through her extensive collection of music records and picked out one containing slow banjo duets partnered with saxophones. The harmonics were loose, borderline lazy, but it was just the petting she needed now. Her gramophone player was a treasured legacy given to her by the town, but it still played like new. Radios seldom had a speaker that could outdo this device no matter how well made they were, at least not yet, and one merely had to adjust the volume to avoid noise complaints.

The music gave her home a dose of playfulness as she fetched a deck of cards from the bedroom to play several rounds of Solitaire, pushing back her crestfallen thoughts for now. Yes, it had to be Krayble's strict methods that had caused matters to languish, to fall cold and violent. Playing alone before crowds had always given her stage fright. Ever since childhood, she'd been nervous to do so, anxious, terrified even, especially if those watching were bodies of threads, with ropes for hair.

Cold water down her back.

Frozen panic—a room full of dolls, the flashes painful, the punishment severe.

A sting of electricity.

Please, stop.

Her hand squeezed the cards, her eyelids pressed shut, her back facing the door towards the living room. Then all at once, the gramophone music died, and a cool draft ran up her clothes. Overcome with surprise, she didn't turn around. If this was anything like before, reacting would only bring a repeat of abhorrent images destined to linger, a carbon copy of recent events thought to have been buried by time.

That being said, she had to look eventually.

Reservations aside, Lola turned slowly. The apartment door was cracked open, strangely, and its mouth breathed in, a breeze gently combing her hair as if wanting to know its texture, its raven-black hue. Perhaps this was a reckless mistake by the maintenance crew, or an apparition trying to sneak in. But that failed to explain why her gramophone player had stopped, the disc unmoving. A wash of worry traveled down her back. This was not the same anxiety from Krayble's tutoring. It was more frantic. It was like an intruder had entered, one with floating footsteps, and apparently, the correct room key.

She placed her cards carefully on the nightstand, then without looking away, bent down to reach under the bed, mentally sighing in relief. The small pepper spray canister was metal, so its cool touch was easy to recognize. Break-ins, while rare in these parts of Strevenfall's townscape, were not unheard of. A few uneasy steps allowed her a full peek across the living room. There was no movement at first, no signs of life, just a soundless vacuum disturbed only by her heartbeat thudding against her rib cage. Then, a near-inaudible noise prompted Lola's gaze downward.

Sallow afternoon rays made the little girl standing there appear trapped within a tawny prism of light. Her small dress was royal blue, and it bloomed as such that it contrasted with everything nearby.

Lola dropped the pepper spray, dumbfounded, a reaction brought on not because of what this child wore, but rather, what was clutched in her hands. She was certain "Hummingbird's Verse" had been jailed inside the violin's coffin, yet here this intruder was, holding it, her young cobalt eyes looking the sheets over with broad, almost loving tenderness.

21

Eyes like hers.

The dress like hers.

The face, the hair color.

Somehow, time had bent backwards. Lola knew who this girl was.

And it couldn't be real.

This had to be fiction, an impossible happenstance, a delusion resulting from a food-deprived body merged with insomnia. Her instincts rejected what she saw but her eyes wouldn't lie, while her mind drew blanks, failing to grasp at logic. A tight, startled gasp escaped her lips. Lola's shock magnified when the little girl peered up at her with eyes that could be likened to wet glass. Perhaps she was welling up with tears. Maybe she herself would well up with tears. The room seemed charged with vertigo, making it hard to breathe, harder to think. But she had to think now, think of a way to act.

"You, don't move!" Lola said finally, choking on the words. She raced back coughing as if her throat was sandpaper. The bathroom greeted her with a mirror reflecting someone who looked utterly terrified. She flung open the medicine cabinet and grabbed a small white bottle of pills that would surely quell the illusion. The instructions demanded that one capsule would suffice. She wolfed down four without water. More were gagged up than swallowed, so she kept gulping until they were gone. She stared widely at the sink drain, arms viced straight against the counter, imagining all her panic swirling down the hole and through the pipes, never to be seen again. She counted—one, two, three, four. Good, everything would go back to normal. Five, six, seven—the pills would work. Eight, nine, ten—it was over. Everything was fine, and tomorrow she would tell Mr. Krayble that yesterday's hysteria had been a fluke.

"Is this yours?"

Lola froze. Peripheral vision confirmed the girl was standing some feet away, and it took every bit of boldness to look at her directly. She was offering the peppery spray, which rested on her palm.

"W-what?"

22

The girl promptly stepped forth, eyes widened. "Oh, I asked if this was yours."

Lola was mute, her breath that of weightless noise, and her eyes were again drawn to "Hummingbird's Verse" held lazily in the girl's other hand, as if it were a toy. Yet ghosts couldn't hold objects, right? Still, she thought it best to act like this intruder was just that, a ghost, a phantom without depth. She knelt warily, her mind reaching out, before reaching physically.

Lola tried taking the music only for the girl to move away.

"Hey!" the girl exclaimed, holding up the spray and pointing at it, pouting. "I was talking about *this*, not that."

"Who…are you? Where did you come from?"

"I guess this spray thing's mine now since you don't want it."

"Please, just tell me how you got here."

"Well thanks for the toy, but Ma's gonna make me give it back anyway, so…I'll just leave it here." The girl reached to set the canister on the sink counter, and after an obviously fake smile, proceeded to exit the bathroom with a trotting skip punctuated by tiny flip flops smacking the carpet. They were white, akin to a snow rabbit's fur. Familiar.

"Wait!"

Soft blue fabric rippled as the girl turned back around, wearing a flustered expression, waiting anxiously. Lola was flustered too, filled with emotion, breath stifled. She knelt on all fours now, inching closer to this new yet familiar child. Remarkably, when her fingertips brushed the hem of her dress, the girl didn't pull back. It was made from velvet, just as expected. Another familiar piece, but one more was needed, one more to confirm this was real, that this wasn't fiction. Reluctantly, she allowed her gaze to drift down towards the girl's hands. Both of them were blotched with bruised skin—fingers and all—beaten, tortured. Their ravaged discoloration made it seem like they'd been stricken with frostbite, brittle to the bone.

"Hey, what happened to your hands?" Lola asked softly, not knowing whether to push this girl away now or to hold her close. The question didn't need answering, though. She knew it already. Perhaps she'd asked just to hear this child's voice again. Perhaps she'd asked just to further realize who this girl was, because the sight of her alone was moving, poignant, and sensitive, to say the least.

"Please, answer me. Why are you here? What happened?"

But like a chemical reaction, a pulse of anger flashed in the girl's eyes. "What do you mean? You know what happened!" She raised "Hummingbird's Verse" with those same discolored hands and proceeded to tear its wings off.

"No!" Lola scrambled to pry the bird from its abuser's grip. It was a vicious back and forth deteriorating quickly into an arduous struggle. The girl squirmed to keep "Hummingbird's Verse" out of reach, arms flailing, legs kicking. Lola winced as a set of nails dug across her shoulder, then cried out when a set of teeth bit into her arm, and she recoiled, the girl wiggling free and sprinting out of the bathroom.

Lola squeezed the wound as blood trickled down her arm, shocked, confused, then angry. A trail of scattered paper bits made it easy to follow the child into the living room again, where she'd first appeared.

But it was too late.

"Hummingbird's Verse" was clutched in the girl's hands, the song maimed, unreadable. Lola stood dumbfounded. "Why would you do that? Where did you come from? Why are you here?" With each unanswered question the girl stepped back, until her heels brushed the wall behind.

"Why do this?" This time Lola quelled her angry tongue in efforts to sound gentle, even though yelling would have felt much better. She knelt so that their eyes could meet more directly. "I just want answers. Understand? That's all. Now, where did you come from?"

The question drowned in silence yet again. Anger swelled once more, threatening to pour from her lips as words of stone, but that would only make things worse. She approached slower than before. A mere foot separated them now.

"It's alright. I...don't want the music anymore." Lola could only say this on good terms because, looking over, she noticed that her violin case had remained shut, meaning her own copy of "Hummingbird's Verse" was still safe within its coffin, guilty as that was. "Please, show me your hands. I won't hurt you, promise."

The girl frowned. "You're lying."

"I'm not."

"Liars always look away when lying."

"I'm not looking away. *You* look injured. I can help you."

"How?"

Lola managed a smile. "Well again, for starters, I can take a look at your hands." She offered her own hands, palms up. "Trust me, I know what it feels like."

After sliding between defiance and unsureness, the girl dropped the last bits of paper, then raised her fingers. The two pairs of hands joined, the bottom one supporting its wounded partner—finally, contact, unrestrained by pain or fear.

"See? I'm not all bad." Lola regarded the bruised skin that had been induced by endless strain, numerous rounds of torture. If she'd applied more pressure, they might've snapped, easily. She wiped an eye to find it on the verge of tears, trying not to shake again. Her vision blurred. A chilled movement rose in her chest, as if a shard was buried there, expanding.

She looked up.

The girl's body was undergoing movement of its own, strange static flickering the edges of her frame, a distortion of reality. She looked to be fading, clothes warping, hair fluctuating between here and not, visible one second, vanished the next, blinking in and out of being, her hands, her face, and her expression grew worried as they peered into Lola's own. And Lola couldn't believe what was happening. Why was this child fading? Why the static glitches in her frame and the flickering madness swallowing her body? The tumult raged, more, more still, the ghostly furor reflecting in

Lola's eyes, through them, swarming her brain with freezing thoughts, fearful, horrifying notions of things never meant to rise.

A sting of electricity.

A wand cracking bone.

A morningtide torture.

And then, in one violet flicker of space, the girl vanished. The music resumed. The door slammed shut. A cool draft went up her clothes.

It was over. The little girl had disappeared.

And Lola sat there, dazed, arms limp, fathoms deep in bewilderment. Each layer of noise and feeling came back in phases, each one weighing down until she felt whole, heavy. Her heartbeat settled after a long painful wait in silence, of racing thoughts and memories sharper than knives.

She lethargically carried on to her bedroom, taking small steps, trying to keep it in just a little longer, long enough to reach the blankets and rest, to absorb what happened, to reprise in peace, finally, peace.

But she made it halfway when the stress within her broke loose, the emotion letting out. She toppled against the wall as her brain flashed white, over, and over…and over again. Everything today had proven arduous. Everything had gone wrong. Everything had brought memories of that which words could not describe.

Please, I've had enough.

And now, everything was granular noise. Her throat quivered. Her eyes pressed shut, and her sobbing disturbed the lighthearted music as it continued playing, but no one else heard. The only other person had vanished, leaving her to be swept away, alone, confused, and frightened.

Hibernal Sleepwalk

"Ambright: the universe where all the realms float about in the cosmos, our home, our past, and our future. From Droodpike, Hobe, Strevenfall, to the outermost regions of space where you'll find the realms of Clodwoo, Zesh, and Typhame. Aezial, meanwhile, is the realm above all others, the first creation in the universe, and the origin of eather, the magic that saturates the skies of most worlds..."

- An introductory lesson given at Garenham University

The echoes of tension dwelled deep in Lola's mind; a tidal flow rife with nightmare-inducing horror. They fell cold between her thoughts like snow where the flashbacks of prior events resonated. The illusions. Were they illusions? The flickering? The girl? She felt ridiculous in her attempts to think about what happened logically, as if reasoning could apply here. Everything had changed without warning.

Now, walls of jars and bottles looked down at her like an audience long dead, watching with placid eyes as she sat in the patient's chair. A man worked behind his frail walnut desk with one hand pinched around a quill feather, scribbling down notes at impossible speeds. It had taken more time than expected to land a doctor's appointment. Few such offices existed within the cityscape surrounding Garenham's school grounds. People were constantly turning up with some kind of viral infection, one of the many drawbacks of living among a dense population. In fact, this town was the largest in Strevenfall, the second largest half its size. So perhaps it was understandable.

Sitting there gave Lola many chances to rethink her circumstances. Perhaps a psychologist or a mage would have been a better fit to remedy this type of sickness, if one even dared call it that. The only proof of what had transpired with the girl were the marks running down her arm and the teeth indentations keeping them company, both tightly bandaged.

She resurfaced from thought when the quill stopped scribbling. The man—a middle-aged elf sporting a beard and curly hair—looked up from his legal pad with a quizzical, concerned countenance.

"And the child...vanished?" he said, brow raised.

Lola gripped her dress. "Even a psycho wouldn't make this up. You have to believe me."

"Miss Pern, the issue I'm having has nothing to do with your authenticity. It's your record." He raised the legal pad and flicked it. "Other than some drinking habits during your late adolescent years, you've been clean since moving to Garenham. No broken bones. No head injuries, nothing. I'm aware that university exams are coming up in a few weeks before the solstice arrives. This could be nothing but stress, in which case I can recommend proper medication. Keep in mind that students always tend to feel—"

"Stress? Stress!" Lola stood and thrust her bitten arm towards the man's face. "Dr. Hane, you've been my go-to expert ever since I moved here. Finals have never caused anything like this!"

"Sit down, please!"

She sat. Both of them sighed.

"Now we can either rush to conclusions, or take this slow, step by step. I can prescribe some of these serotonin reuptake inhibitors to combat dips in cognitive function. In other words, they will help you focus." Dr. Hane rose to scan a few of the shelves with his fingertips, touching over the glass and plastic bottles until he stopped at a dark blue vial covered in white scripting.

Lola was handed the vial with a paper strand stapled to its lid, and after reading the fine print, her eyes widened.

"An issue, I presume?"

"The side effects include drowsiness...during the day? I'm tired as it is! Surely there's a way to divvy up the pills over time."

"Very well. I can draw it out over three months at most. Just don't overdose, and always take it before bed." Dr. Hane slipped open a drawer and pushed an unfilled sheet across his desk. "All I need now are a few signatures. Believe me, Miss Pern, the last thing I want is to see you under any kind of stress. It's vital to work bottom up instead of rushing things. Give it a week. If this ends up being ineffective, or if you have any allergic response, let me know, and we'll try something else."

Lola walked out with a paper bag and a weekly checkup schedule. The morning's powder-gray aura doused the buildings, brought by rain clouds yet to spill their payload. She felt hollowed out, as if the next breeze could sweep her up and carry her body several blocks ahead, or perhaps an updraft would lift her towards the stratosphere. Her newfound exhaustion hinted at insomnia; a punishment likely received following the recent trauma.

At Sandy's Diner, a boiling water pot dribbled across the stove, sizzling, and her heart leapt. She'd been waist deep in thought again, going about tasks in a predisposed state of being where everything happened somewhere far away. The steam cooker emitted soft vapor plumes about her face. It was soothing, a sauna for her skin, but the comfort left when someone tapped her shoulder.

"We have a real looker up front—broad shoulders and decent pythons to match." Iris didn't have her ponytail this morning, hair flowing down like streams of amber in a way that exposed the woman's surprising youth.

Lola decided to play along. Doing so would be a welcome distraction from distant thoughts going nowhere. "So, it's a guy this time," she said.

"Does he come here often? Lots of new students arrive this time of year to prepare for the next semester."

"A new student? Doesn't look like it. The guy looks just your age, and in my opinion, just your type."

"The matchmaker, are you?"

Iris laughed and pointed over the steaming griddles. "We still have a couple of waitresses' uniforms on the rack, you know, if you want to socialize."

Lola glanced over and dared not imagine how she'd look wearing one—a black and white dress with many pieces that could easily be misarranged. "Alright, but managers have the final word," she said.

Iris straightened up and pointed onward, grinning. "Then here's my word, then. I hereby command that you take the guy's order. Oh, and he's human like you are, so he's hard to miss."

She grinned despite the cheesy antics, not because of her friend's playfulness, but solely from the fact that she'd taken the offer to go up front and commune with the customers. A sojourn away from cookers and stoves seemed refreshing.

Interestingly enough, gathering a few bold nerves took longer than changing. She walked idly into the open rows of booths and tried mimicking the rhapsody other staff wore on their faces, only to come up short. She settled with a lean smile as a cheaply forged mock-up, sweeping tight glances until she caught a man seated at a vacant table—human, just like Iris had said. Flirting wasn't a foreign concept to her, but she'd never done so wearing a costume.

Come on Iris. You know people hook up in bars more than restaurants.

"Alright, so what can I get for you today?" Lola flipped out a small notepad and pen. Sure, the guy was handsome, but she was too caught up in writing down his order to weave anything extra in between, not a tease, nothing.

Then, as if recalling a joke, the man looked up from his menu, eyes filled with something between surprise and amusement.

30

"Oh, come on," she said, lips stretching. "I don't look *that* ridiculous."

"You...you're the one, aren't you?" He replied, obviously amused. "The one who fled Krayble's auditorium several weeks ago."

The pen stopped between words. Lola was suddenly cold, struggling to keep her heart from catching on surprise. "You mistake me for someone else," she replied, nearly in a whisper. "There's many who look like me."

"You must be joking. I'm not seeing any fins or pointed ears. You're human like me."

Lola's yearning to object was met with hesitation. Nothing could be said to push away the truth when it clung like cellophane. So, there she stood, left with an answer unspoken. "Sir, your order remains unfinished."

But the man didn't cooperate. "Some people think you had a panic attack. Was it the song you were playing? It couldn't have been from our handouts. Was it extra credit?"

Some of her anger slipped. "You don't stop, do you?"

"Sorry?"

"Listen, I'd rather not be told about yesterday, and it's clear you're done ordering. The food will arrive shortly." A few spotlights turned as she hurried back to the kitchen area. Inside, she leaned against the back wall and sighed, watching steam clouds rise from the grills as they droned on, speaking their subtle, hissing tongues. She drew in these sounds and endeavored to make a song from them, a tranquil rhythm to alleviate the cold collected in her mind.

Iris came over, the song dispersing.

"I just overreacted a little," Lola said. "My order's easy, though he was still a bit prying once I jotted everything down. Let's skip the extra socializing for today. Sound fair?" She stood tiredly and stuck her paper on the vegetable cooker. "But it's *not* fair leaving his order incomplete. I'll prepare and serve the food myself once I change clothes."

"Oh, I see," Iris nodded.

"It's...my fault really. I'll be back in a minute."

31

She relaxed finally when the bathroom door closed. The noise outside came like a soft rumble, easy to ignore. After changing back into her cooking attire, she arranged the meal and returned up front with a tray balanced on her hand. Some turned at her arrival, some curious, others unfazed, but she was focused on the man. His eyes lifted when she sat the tray down and began setting its contents in their proper places.

"No dress?"

Lola's eyes merely brushed his own. "I made the order myself. I had to change."

"Oh." He paused. "My name's Axel, by the way."

"Listen, what happened last time was just me overreacting."

His brow raised. "Honestly, I don't blame you. I attended Krayble's seminar last year. His methods are impossible sometimes. I wouldn't take it much to heart."

"Well, it's good you don't blame me, because I wanted to ask you something." She leaned in and lowered her voice just out of whisper territory. "How many people know? I mean, about what happened there."

He leaned in too, perhaps mocking her. "How would you react if I said, the whole music wing of Garenham University?"

Lola didn't react. Her skin on her neck prickled as if ice was pressed against it. This had been a mistake. She'd offered a question that would likely worsen matters if the conversation continued. More spotlights had swiveled in her direction. People were watching her, watching them.

Cold water down her back.

"Great. That's just…great." Her voice thinned, the words starved mid-sentence. It was best if she'd turn around and walk off, perhaps with kind nods to those she'd pass. So that's what she did. Dolls were found across the floor with jointless arms and twisted bodies, their faces built from yarn, buttons, threaded lifelessness, although no one else seemed to notice them. Pain flared from her bandaged arm where the girl's teeth had dug into it, pain that had been rising and fading over the past week, but right now she couldn't do much beyond shoving it aside.

32

At her station again, particles of misty droplets hugged her pores and soothed them. Many on campus knew what had transpired yesterday, a heavy burden of truth. The infection would spread. More spotlights would swivel her way, more attention she didn't want.

A sting of electricity.

A wand cracking bone.

A smoking rod.

After pressing through work's final hours, she returned home on foot rather than by carriage. Doing so created a lapse of time keen to distractions, anything to get lost in thought. A few minutes would do—the feeling of solace within one's mind. She paced near a ballroom blaring its piano-saxophone duet. She thought about having a try at some dumb fun. However, keeping a three-year streak free of alcohol was much more impressive than being passed out on the counter. There was so much to lose back then, when she was younger, when she was more vulnerable to peer pressure.

Some other time, maybe.

The apartment's mouth clicked shut. Strangely, Lola expected her living room to be dense with overturned clutter, to find the girl standing there again. Yet her shadow stretched across nothing more than carpet. The silence brought memories of what had transpired then, so she flipped through her collection and picked a vinyl disc that held many layers of sound and rhythm. The music left sparse room for thoughts dealing with times prior, and thankfully, sleep was only a short way off. Walking home had drained most of the early night's hours, pallid stars speckling above the clouds, the clouds blocking most of them. Her bones felt heavy, drowsiness welcomed like a pleasant visitor from lands of mystery. It was time she swallowed Dr. Hane's remedy for nightmares.

In the bathroom, she tore the paper bag with tired eagerness, revealing what would hopefully be an answer to this whimsical illness, this narrative hailstorm. In one anxious breath she spun off the bottle cap, rolled out a pill, and swallowed it dry. Her face hung over the sink drain, hair spilling over the sides of her face like a raven-colored curtain. If there was even a speck of relief to be had now, she wanted to readily embrace it. Perhaps it would come in waves, or in one continuous flow of serenity, or even a single wash of joy. She waited patiently, motionlessly, hopefully.

Nothing came. It was just medicine, after all.

A sharp contrast of red and silver bled into the side of her vision. Lola grabbed the pepper spray, but she didn't focus on it. The bitter memory surrounding it would only make things worse. She tossed the canister under the bed and climbed on top, allowing the mattress to absorb her payload of weary limbs. "Hummingbird's Verse" was absent from the stand this time, still locked away where no one could find it. By now, the coffin had garnered a thin coat of dust, a sign of her regretful yet purposeful reluctance to interact with her violin, to play its music. On normal occasions, she'd be practicing out on the hillsides with a bold moon watching down from its starry throne, wearing her royal blue sundress, reacting to every shift of air, every slight breeze that brushed her skin, every blade of grass swaying as she herself swayed in effortless twirls, going around in wide pivots as her flats caressed the dance floor, the ground. Then, as all seemed delightful, the tremolo would come and abruptly force everything to a standstill.

It was like a predetermined instinct. No matter how much effort was put into playing the song perfectly, she'd always stumble. The tremolo wasn't even the hardest part in "Hummingbird's Verse". In fact, the technique itself existed within other musical works she'd already mastered years ago. And weeks ago, this tremolo within "Hummingbird's Verse" hadn't even been an issue.

But now, things were different.

The music's cursed by a ghost, she thought teasingly. *I'm set to tell Dr. Hane that my problems are caused by a poltergeist.*

Music, different music, continued playing from her living room, filling every bit of space necessary so that she didn't have to think much else about anything.

Just listen.

Relax.

Forget.

I can't forget.

Move on.

I can't move on.

I can't...forgive.

...forgive.

For a while Lola was buried under every intricate noise, separating each layer of sounds to their fundamental roots, lost. Then her mind wandered towards an image that seemed blurred at first but sharpened after a moment's passing. The guy from Sandy's Diner had worn a suit, though not opulent in the slightest. It had been made of silk, and subtly colorful—purple?—with a flower stitched to its collar. A dancer's uniform? Perhaps, perhaps not. His eyes had been a gray hazel blend of exotic proportions, like a pair of storm clouds.

"Oh, and that ridiculous top hat," she whispered, and chuckled lightly. "Oh dear."

Showering would have to wait until morning, because doing so now would only swell her drowsiness, and she'd likely fall asleep on the porcelain bed. That is, until the cold water would agitate her to waking. She breathed tiredly and rolled on her back, sprawling out with arms stretched across the sheets, looking up with tired eyes. The ceiling looked back. It and she had a staring contest to see who would blink first.

"Fine, you win." Her eyelids gave out. The pill's added melatonin was too heavy to resist.

The Great Inner Snowglobe

"A realm once torn apart, now held together by massive pillars running through the earth. Strevenfall has been caught up in more wars than one can count, but now, hardened by those conflicts, it has become one of the most peaceful realms in Ambright."

- Heron

Lola was gradually lifted from her dreams by a soft, steady murmur soaking through her pillow. The bedroom window revealed Strevenfall's sky drowning amid an unforgiving storm front. Rain poured like curtains. Far off, gentle booms of thunder chased their lightning counterparts. For a long time she peered through the glass while her body thawed its rigid outer coat, waking up slowly. A new week had turned, meaning classes would resume in full swing. Krayble's afternoon block was last on her schedule, but honestly, it didn't matter what course or lecture she would take part in. Almost everyone knew about her supposed deluded panic. Almost everyone knew how much she'd buckled, how she reacted when others watched her fail.

A different noise disturbed the weather's muttering, breaking her time in peaceful limbo. Weighted with apathy, she walked over to peek towards

36

the living room's mouth. The door sounded like it was being hammered by an angry pair of fists, pounding against her ears, demanding entry.

Or perhaps they were actually fists.

"Please, not now," she mumbled, as if doing so would quell the racket. The door pounded again, louder. She checked her state of dress and was reminded that it hadn't changed since yesterday—a pale sundress. Her hair told a different story, but its unruliness could wait.

She flung open the door, but it wasn't the girl. It was a woman she knew from down the hall.

"What is it?"

"What is it?" The woman's glare sharpened, and she pointed at her. "It was playing all night! Your little orchestra in a box didn't let me sleep 'till morning!"

Lola turned where her gramophone spun even though its vinyl had gone mute hours ago. "Well, why didn't you tell me sooner?"

"I tried, lady, but you were dead to the world. Someone like you might be used to it, but not me, and not most of this building." She flicked her watch and grunted. "And now I've overslept. Just remember our conversation, alright?"

Lola pushed the door shut. Her thoughts wavered between euphoria and discord, herself drowning in vertigo. Dr. Hane's treatment felt to be working, however. She was rested and focused, awake more than ever, but still remained less so compared to weeks prior—before things had worsened. And there wasn't a pill in existence that could dissolve the upcoming spotlights at Garenham. The embarrassment itself would inevitably pass over time, but not the way others would see her now, seeing her in a new, unfamiliar way. They would see a musician who was frightened of crowds, and whose esteemed reputation among teachers had fallen somewhat. They would pity her.

"Pity," she muttered, spitting the word from her lips like rotten food. "Pity—as if that were the case growing up."

Mother.

Father.

A wand cracking bone.

A smoking rod.

A sleepless night.

A young marigold sun burned cracks between the clouds, and where rain fell beneath them, they glinted like stardust. Puddles rippled to the downpour, reflecting distorted images of Lola traveling along the sidewalk, along soaked paths of concrete and around narrow street corners. Though her shoes might be waterlogged, the dark blue umbrella she carried on days like this kept the shower's touch away from her clothing. A pair of gemstones dangled from either ear, short silver chains ending off with teardrop lapis lazulies. She enjoyed the fashion sometimes, other times not, but this time any jewelry might have been counterproductive. Drawing attention wasn't exactly the goal today.

Should've left them back home.

Lola stopped at the curb, waiting for the sound of wheels crunching on loose gravel and dirt. In the morning hours just before the sun had fully risen, carriages were heard long before they were seen. Less of them made rounds during the early hours, so the wait was longer. But that was fine. She wanted nothing more now than to be enveloped within the rain's mollifying harmony, watching water drops drizzle off her umbrella and descend. Across the street, a lonely streetlamp spilled its gold-crusted gloom over the road, but dwindled before the light could reach her.

The familiar clopping noise echoed, and she waved the carriage over. The ride was quiet.

Thankfully, few roamed the campus grounds this early—just a small handful of scholars with books and tablets pouched under their arms. Coverlets of fog hovered low across the dew-drenched grass; a velvet mist laden about her feet as she hurried inside to escape the weather. A passing of gray and hollow white sun filtered through the stained-glass roofs, dousing every tenement and hall with a colorless aura. The great ivory columns holding everything up had a sickly presence about them, lacking their daily bath of hues soaring through the spectrum.

Lola's first block was an orchestra theory course held in one of the smaller auditoriums. A circular space of rows stacked twenty times over, it could accommodate quite a few people, but the early class was small and most sat up front. She merely glanced at their faces upon entering. A few spotlights swiveled in her direction.

Cold water down her back.

She took her seat.

She took out her notes.

She took a deep breath, blinked, and dipped under the flow of attachment, sentencing herself to a state of repose where unwanted sounds resonated as static whispers, too far away. Maintaining this form proved somewhat easy. All it required was one small step back into the corners of the mind, watching everything unfold through a distant, dream-like view.

The hours droned by and were unbearable, each one dragging its feet, seemingly moving at their own pace. More people arrived on campus as dawn bled into morning, then morning into midday. Between classes, if people stared, they were ignored. If people whispered, their voices were smothered and drowned out by her secluded mindfulness. Not all of them reacted, though. Some turned a blind eye, but in reality, the fact that even some looked was too much, because all of this had been derived from one tragic accident without cause, one slip where everybody could see.

She glanced down. Perhaps it was the shallow breaks along her forearm that had drawn her attention—reddened notches across her skin where the girl had bitten. The bandages had been removed so that her skin could breathe, exposing the wound, scabbed, slightly swollen. Touching it always proved a mistake no matter how brash her curiosity grew. Pain flared and prickled at the slightest pressure, yet her tunneled focus dared not leave such curiosity behind. Her thoughts adhered to every second as to make every second feel longer, her body somehow colder, and now, strangely, her head started aching too, a slow methodical pound like a drum beating louder every few minutes, then every minute.

She pushed it away.

She needed to focus on what the professor was saying—jotting down notes, recording lessons from previous group exercises, personal work, class critiques. Yet such tasks were starting to feel impossible, the feeling in her arm greater. Outside, the morning's rain had lifted, sunlight slicing through the storm clouds, tearing them apart.

By afternoon's arrival, her head was a cauldron of swirling throbs with no sign of fading. Her focus couldn't venture from this new form of strain, these thoughts pulsing like a secondary heartbeat moving in her skull, like a force trying to escape.

Lola stood before a veil of thick wooden slabs. Krayble's auditorium was just beyond these doors, a funeral hall with seats for gravestones, where her dignity had died. At least, that's what she'd conjured things up to be, dramatic as it was. Tension crawled up her spine and spoke in a chilled voice of recency. Her feet refused to budge from their placement on the marble even though she'd commanded them to work. Parts of her wanted this to be over. Other parts wanted this to have never begun.

The great slabs opened to release its throng of students dismissed from class. Lola watched them leave like watching a fog envelope then flow past her—a continuous surge of bodies bumping and weaving all around her, herself unmoving. She'd soon have to move, though, lest she be stared at for imitating an ice sculpture. But the only reason she moved at all was a light tap on her shoulder, alongside a vaguely familiar voice.

"Someone seems out of it. Everything alright?"

Her senses snapped into focus when it registered who the voice belonged to. It was quite the surprise. Axel's stylized attire was that of a garnet silk suit and top hat, clothes that normally found their homes on entertainers, not the musical type. His eyes expressed a focused clarity that drew her attention towards them, until he blinked, and her attention once again landed on his words.

"Oh, it's you again," Lola said. "Where'd you come from?"

He paused, curious. "Fresh out of chorus class like the others. You didn't see me walking up to you?"

"No...no I suppose not." She clamped her forearm, as if letting go would set off an avalanche.

"So, everything's *not* alright?"

She moved away.

"Wait! I wanted to apologize for yesterday."

His words locked in her ears more than words should have, and the cobalt in her eyes sharpened. "That's a pretty strange thing to say. Believe me, I'm the one who should be apologizing."

"Oh? Then I'm at a loss." Axel neared her so that their voices could lower. "To my memory, it was me who first brought up your predicament yesterday at the diner. It seemed you became troubled when I asked about it." He flipped off his hat and bowed slightly. "And to that, my apologies."

She nodded after regarding him carefully. "Well, if that's all, my next class starts any time now. You know Mr. Krayble doesn't believe in excused absences."

"But miss, if I may be observant, you don't seem to have an instrument."

She suddenly noticed the hollow absence of weight in her hand, an emptiness buried under the day's pressure. True enough, she'd left her violin to collect more dust back home.

Her headache drummed louder.

Louder.

Louder still.

"Miss, are you certain everything's alright? You look pale, and that's saying a lot." Axel reached out.

"Fine! Just fine!" Lola pulled back and started rushing towards the seminar. "Krayble has spare violins around back. Don't waste your time fussing over me." She bustled inside, teeth clattering. Even if Mr. Krayble had wanted to look her way, she wouldn't return the favor. Her head and forearm pulsed with crushing waves upon waves of pain, rising through her body, her bones. The storage room was a marble chamber with enough shelves to house more than twice its contents. She stopped before the entrance. Another pair of footsteps had been trailing behind.

"I said not to follow me."

Axel leaned forward. "You need a nurse."

"I told you I'm fine!"

"You're shivering like crazy."

Lola winced as she pulled a case from the top shelf, a viola, not a violin, but she knew it was easier to play. "Fine, since you won't leave me alone, I'll just prove it. How about I play some dumb song to show you I'm healthy?" Dizziness filled her head once she pulled the instrument from its case. She could hardly hold the bow right, gripping it so tight her fingers paled. "Just let me finish and...and then you can...leave."

Louder.

A deafening sound broke the air in two, high, crackling, painful. She'd snapped the bow by accident, her tight hold on it enough that it crunched like an icicle. Red trails moved down her arm, her hand splintered horribly.

Louder.

Louder.

Louder than the bow snapping was her head, snapping in and out of focus.

Just let me finish and...and then you can...leave...

Leave...can you then and...and finish me let just...

Finish me...

You can...leave.

Louder.

A smoking rod.

A sleepless night.

An endless cycle.

There was a flatline in the atmosphere where her tide of consciousness receded, allowing something far more enigmatic to seep into her thoughts, freezing there. She looked up expecting Axel. Axel wasn't there, just a ruined tapestry where everything had blurred. The world was an indistinct mess of color blotted through reality. Everything had vanished. Everyone was gone.

A cool whirl of air rustled her clothes. Like a serpent it coiled around Lola's body, as if to know her shape, her damage. Something washed around her feet, her toes, submerging them. It was water, water with salty crests swirling around like clouds. Another breeze lifted her hair as she looked around. An endless plane of flat ocean fanned out towards a boundless horizon, every direction swallowed by liquefied sheets of glass, and she stood right in the midst of it, dazed, as if dreaming.

"Hey! Is anyone here!" The vastness swallowed her voice. A violent gust blew and she fell back with her arm bleeding, her hand stinging as salt water bathed the open wound. She held the arm tightly as pain soaked it through, teeth gritting.

"Help!"

Again, no one answered. As she rose, stumbling, a fleck of dust landed in front of her eyes, but it moved when she looked elsewhere. It wasn't dust. A pin-sized grain protruded from the skyline, a black dot hardly visible across the shallow, flattened water. Perhaps it hadn't been there before, or maybe overwhelming panic had made her blind to such details. Either way, something was there, and within this sudden illusion of sorts, it was the only sign of direction.

"Where...am I?"

The sea of glass wrinkled as Lola trekked through in caution. Oceanic whispers told her ears that something ought to be familiar. The dot gradually expanded while her passage left a long, winding wake. More whispers paid their visits, carrying with them a scent that brought déjà vu, but she was still lost for what they said. Still, her hand and forearm throbbed heavily. Schools of angelfish sailed beneath the water's face. A baby seahorse paused to watch her feet stir up plumes of sediment.

Indeed, an ocean.

Closer in, she realized the speck was a house, a structure made from ramshackle wood rotted smooth by endless surf.

"What's this doing here?" Lola whispered. The front door was on the verge of collapsing when she opened it. Inside, flooded rooms waited with their torn curtains and picture frames, everything long since disheveled by age. Her fingers trailed along the hallway wall as she peered into the empty spaces forgotten by time. Clothes were piled on tables and carpet. Each room was a body starved of people. Each room held furniture floating on the water. Each room delivered sharp feelings of remembrance.

One room had a dresser with cavities where drawers used to be, and a rocking chair sitting idly near a corner. Her eyes moved back to the dresser. On top of it were photos trapped in silver frames, the photos themselves undamaged.

She held one up against the sunlight and wiped off its dusty layer of grime, squinting at two fuzzy shapes sitting together. After a long pause, her eyes widened with shock.

"My parents," her voice trailed, and she looked around. "My parents' house."

The world flickered and tore back history. The sky suddenly changed from topaz to an amethyst dusk, the dreamworld descending towards an earlier point in time, floors rippling, walls cascading with a mystic energy transcendent of nature. Apparitions morphed into existence, and like ghosts their figures were translucently dull. Now, a woman sat in the rocking chair with her narrowed gaze directed towards a stack of sheet music. Elsewhere, a scrawny man wearing a flannel jacket blew another puff of smoke from his pipe, regarding the woman absently through his monocle.

"Mother...Father?" When Lola managed to thaw from her initial state of shock and call to them, her voice fell on deaf ears.

A phonograph player sang next to a candlelit nightstand. The man's nimble hand threw off its needle to usher in silence. "Evelyn dear, our little one's already performed those singles over and over again. She is ready for harder material."

"Not quite, Calvik," Evelyn answered in her own time. "I still see where the tutor critiqued her etude assignments. I know they are only short compositions, but there's no excuse. There's also no excuse for skipped notes and off-played tunes, especially at her level."

Lola knew they spoke of her, yet neither seemed able to see her standing there in plain view. She wanted to reach for them, but her thoughts were tangled up with so many questions, so many concerns.

How did I get here?

What happened?

Why?

"Maybe it's best we cancel her play date with Yercy tomorrow," Evelyn added, holding up a sheet with the words, 'improvement needed', scribbled on top. "She still has trouble transitioning the high partials between measures." Her thin white fingers brushed invisible dust off the paper, then she promptly set them aside. "Calvik, stop smoking and write a note to the tutor requesting an extra visit. Her methods have been doing wonders lately."

Lola watched Calvik pen the message out with a quill feather, sentencing her to another four hours of discipline, another grueling exercise session where every mistake was met with harsh punishment. Anger began its journey through her lungs, as if they'd filled with acid.

Before it flowed past her lips, however, stringed music echoed from downstairs.

Calvik's feather died, the man's brows furrowed. *"That* song again?"

"Unfortunately." Evelyn's voice had turned hard and frigid. "She thinks playing it off and on will make us not notice."

"I assumed she had her scale sheet to practice today—must've already learned it with free time to spare."

Evelyn only offered him a frozen glare.

"Yes dear—when there's room for improvement, free time is a trivial virtue. I'll fetch the rod and head downstairs."

"Please, no." Lola's whisper was aimed not only at her father, but also the one who was sure to be downstairs. She hurried past Calvik, nearing the door farthest down the main hallway. Strangely, while her presence couldn't be seen or heard by others, she could still move the door, cracking it open and slipping through before he saw. She marveled at her frighteningly ghost-like qualities.

The downstairs room was a crucible of sewn bodies, a small circular space shelved with dolls upon dolls filling the area, rows and rows of moppets, marinates, and matryoshkas. Only a small window towards the back wall broke up this haphazard cluster with its dull, pallid glow. Appallment tightened her limbs, though not because these dolls gazed at her directly. No, their plastic eyes were titled down where the little girl sat with her violin, the girl from before, the girl whose familiarity brought equal parts stress and tenderness.

Laden with doubt, Lola paused before stepping any closer, then decided it was best to make sure. "Hey, can you hear me?"

The girl stood and whipped around to face Lola. It was obvious fear had taken her for some time now. She looked panicked, apprehended, fearfully alert. She touched her neck as if expecting something to be pressed there.

"You again!" Her voice was tight with worry. "Go away! Pa's gonna see you and punish me. Or worse, Ma will come and do it herself!"

Lola knelt, hands reaching out as if to calm a mistreated animal, careful not to make any sudden movements or sounds. "You...you remember, don't you?" She looked her over, at her bruise-covered hands and the tired circles rimming her eyes like dark crescent moons.

The girl was mute.

"Please answer me. You have to remember what happened that day. You must remember me." Lola's voice climbed desperately. "You gave me the pepper spray and said—"

"I don't know what happened, alright!" The girl moved away. "I was out playing with Yercy when I suddenly fell asleep. Next thing I know, I'm in a big apartment and a big version of me is living in it." She looked to her music stand. "You really wanted me to hand over that song for some reason."

Sure enough, "Hummingbird's Verse" rested on the stand, the short stack of paper free of correction notes and markings that would have been the result of scrutiny. Lola presumed the song had been torn to shreds when they first met, yet here it was with all its notes and ledgers intact. "That song…" She leaned in, placing her hands on the girl's shoulders. "Tell me, were you playing it just now before I came in? I could hear you upstairs."

She shook her head no at first, but then changed to nodding yes.

"Then, you're expecting…"

Another quiet yes.

"I'm so, so sorry."

The door creaked open. A pipe hung from Calvik's mouth, ash-filled plumes rising to choke the ceiling. "Who were you talking to? The tutor left practice work that needs to be mastered by tonight."

"Look Pa!" The girl pointed. "It's the lady from my dream! The one I met, remember?"

"There is no time for conjuring imaginary friends and putting blame on them. You know how everyone feels about you slacking off." He regarded "Hummingbird's Verse" and sighed. "And you know how your mother feels about you playing that song."

"I was already done with everything else," she muttered.

"Don't talk back to me. You've misbehaved. You know that song serves only as a distraction."

Lola's brewing anger turned to worry as her father puffed another tar cloud. He reached for a device tucked between two dolls, previously hidden by their folded limbs. It was a can-sized contraption almost comically made, a patch-worked mess of wires and wood, with a long metal rod jutting from its rectangular base.

"You know the procedure," Calvik said. "Now be still."

Lola stepped back into a nearby shadow, afraid just like the girl, who couldn't step back.

Calvik stuck the device's nose against the girl's abdomen. A quick stream of volts channeled through her, ripping through her bones. The surrounding puppets and figurines watched silently from their shelves, their blatant, almost calm presence mocking the situation as her small body jerked back in pain. But she stayed submissive despite the affliction. Resisting would only be rewarded with another shock.

"Remember, misbehavior means three days' seclusion upstairs," Calvik said. "It could mean an empty dinner plate, or no light of day for a week. Remember, little one, you mustn't waste time."

The stones he threw weren't idle threats, for they had all come to pass many times before. Here, everyday wrongdoings were dealt with by her mother's reprimand, and every incomplete note or musical phrase resulted in hard swift punishment ranging from containment to starvation. Errors were not welcomed, ever.

Lola turned away.

"We're proud of your perfection, little one, not your mistakes."

The girl yelped again as another sting tightened her skin, stabbing her muscles, going through them like hot pins. The shock didn't last long, but an instant was more than enough time for the pain to linger minutes after. The oddly shaped tool glinted like a monster's wink in her father's hands as light traces of smoke emitted from the rod. Every subsequent shot proved worse than the one before as the metal shaft grew hotter, and hotter.

Lola watched the sequence repeat like an unsympathetic metronome, noticing the girl's eyes wet with tears.

"Please, no more," Lola whispered.

"Please, no more," the girl whispered.

Calvik backed away and watched her like he watched most of everything, an apathetic observer indifferent to others.

"Now assume correct playing posture," he said in a tuneless mutter. "Start with your high scales and work your way down. You'll be done by nightfall."

The girl refused to cry. Crying wasn't allowed here.

Lola was horrified at the scene before her, a scene that had suddenly stopped. Everything and everyone was motionless, caught like statues that flickered and vibrated with that same mystic energy from before.

Her body quivered under the strain of the moment, left to regard this torturous act of reprimand caught in still-frame.

She squeezed her eyes shut until they hurt. When she allowed light to flood back in, she was still inside the same doll room in the abandoned house, only there were no dolls, no Calvik, and no girl. It was just a gutted chamber with two feet of water in it. It was history. It was the past now aged into the future. Putting more thought to it left more questions and confusion than Lola could manage right at the moment. It was frightening—so unbelievably frightening—to be swallowed up, spit out somewhere far away, and forced to see, from the outside, what her days were like back then, without knowing how she ended up there to begin with.

Without explanation.

Without direction.

"I need to escape," Lola told herself, and repeated the phrase in her mind until it stuck there like an inner mantra. She stumbled through the desolate maze of rooms that now moved in disorienting paths, like an abstract jigsaw puzzle. Walls were bending. Windows cracked on their own. The world was breaking apart.

Her expression became washed with terror when she finally found the door and swung it open. The once turquoise sea was a blood-red expanse with dead aquatic life floating on top. But then the water caved in upon itself, leaving a pit of black, nothingness spanning forever.

Light stung her eyes when she regained consciousness. Voices rang through the white wall; a deafening wave. Axel held her head stable as she lay on the floor. Amid the audience peering down at her, Mr. Krayble's spotlight shined the brightest by far. People asked questions. Each one's voice was a different noise pouring past her ears and filling her brain. Their noises merged into a single thread of nausea.

"Everyone back where they were!" Krayble waved the audience away and knelt at Lola's side, adopting a softer tone. "I already requested a nurse who'll escort you to medical care. Please, tell me what's going on."

"A nurse…" Lola's head spun like a broken carousel. "Oh…oh no, I'm already getting treatment from Dr. Hane. I…I have to go…I can't…go yet, but…"

"You're still out of it. Just take it easy until help arrives." The elf's eyes narrowed as if he was examining a puzzle.

How do I explain something like this? Lola thought, tired, aching, hardly able to speak, let alone stand.

"I'm sorry," was all she said, and she sat up, hands wrapped around her face while her hair spilled over the sides, blocking everyone from view. At least this way light couldn't penetrate her eyes. The commotion died around her. Above her, Mr. Krayble looked down. Behind her, a nightmare of her childhood lingered. A calm returned through her mind as she forcibly ignored everything and everyone, all the sounds and motion from outside her veil, but the resulting silence hardly proved a relief.

Faerie

"Anything you can think of with your imagination probably exists somewhere in Ambright, along with anything you can't."

- Sigit; a resident of Chimera's Playpen

"How do you feel right now?"

"Tired, I think. My hand still hurts. My head hurts more."

"What were you doing before this happened?"

"Going to class. Or at least thinking about going to class."

"Why were you just thinking about it?"

"Something happened before. It's a long story."

"Alright, so what can you tell me about that?"

Lola's mouth pursed, as if witnessing a phantom's approach. The room had seemingly become haunted with tension. Gooseflesh rose on her arms. "I blacked out because the pain was unbearable. That's when my dream began, only I was still fully aware of everything going on, like I'd never fallen asleep to begin with." She fidgeted, lacing and unlacing her fingers, looking away. "This all sounds ridiculous, doesn't it?"

"It sounds like you need to be sent home. Here, take this with plenty of water," the nurse said, handing her a small packet, "and get *plenty* of rest."

It was a kick in the teeth, being sent away with more pills and a note saying these illusory syndromes were fake, a mere imbalance, a circumstantial tumult.

But truly, who could blame them?

Would I blame myself?

Do I blame myself?

During the week after, Lola's relationship with time steadily became more obscured. She took long walks back from Sandy's Diner, stopping at lone benches to absorb the night's pleasant concert of stray cats and crickets. The streetlamps glowed like spirits trapped in steel cages. Being drenched with aimless notions made her temporarily forget all the calamity that fear had brought, like surrealism through her bloodstream. She waited for something to come, anything to make it to where her mind needn't marry itself to reality. Each day was spectral. Every second ticked by with apprehension.

She often roused in the dead of night expecting the girl again, only to find nothing. At one moment, her inner clock might have been affected by banshees, the likes of which these current drugs wouldn't alleviate.

Lola shoved another empty pill bottle back over the desk, asking again if Dr. Hane had any magic cure for her symptoms. He offered a vial of dark blue tonic and warned of its side effects, pushing it across the table alongside diet recommendations.

She hurried home and ignored those watching her bustle down the sidewalk. The medicine smelled of vinegar and its taste was just as bitter, but it wasn't working. It merely provoked the disappointment and worry flooding her head. Treatments for dream-like trauma were as helpful as chasing ghosts through walls. She hurled the bottle hard, the mirror shattering and killing her reflection.

What was I doing when this started? The question hung like a wraith as she lay in bed that night. Perhaps recording her events in a journal would be useful. After all, memories kept only in the mind were prone to vanishing.

She grabbed some paper and wrote an exhaustive log containing all she could remember during her time unconscious, notating everything from the grand ocean expanse to the old barren house. Thinking back to what happened made her feather quill waver as she worked quickly, fearing the loss of detail. She also described the time frame extensively—what occurred before and after the nightmare. Soon, Lola had inscribed ten pages of meticulous detail, a testament that could be referred to when memory failed. Her sapphire gaze swept over the lines in search of gaps or breaks in continuity.

Then she leaned back and pressed her tired eyes shut. *I just want to sleep...It doesn't matter how long.*

Fear of being plagued with past eidolons kept her from saying much to anyone, as if those phantoms had become figments of a fabled realm. She longed for coherence, and it consumed her. Anything else was merely a far-off delusion in her mind, better thought of as fiction than something she needed to interact with. The town might have as well been a fairyland of never-ending stories, and Garenham made of pixie dust. She pretty much opted out of future classes—at least for now.

One day, Iris walked up to her. "I hear what people are saying. Is there anything I can do?"

"Please, don't worry. I'm figuring it out."

Lola's first task after returning home was to record any abnormalities. Dull threads of pain still coiled within her. Her brain was an asylum, and her thoughts were prisoners. The gramophone played. The clock needle twitched.

Lola arrived home the next day wearing clothes soaked with water. Thinking only of what happened in the past prevented her from noticing the rain as it pummeled the sidewalks. She was losing touch, partially, gradually feeling more and more strayed from reality. It was a sign. It had to be. And when the familiar throbbing pulsed in her head, it was only a matter of time until the past would haunt her again.

Her body flickered like a ghost's, fading in, fading out.

The world gave way.

Water lifted between her toes.

Cloudy skies formed above.

Waveless glass spread before a seemingly endless horizon, and she stood right in the heart of it again. Finding the tiny black speck proved easier this time. It hadn't moved from its spot sunk into the sand.

Lola headed that way and covered the distance quicker than last time, but before she reached her destination, she stopped, her eyes widened, confused. Another speck had risen eastward, this one smaller than its partner straight ahead. A second house? A second portal leading to somewhere different?

Both?

She trekked on, making the new speck grow in size, its shape becoming clearer with every step and its color emerging with every hard breath scraping her lungs. This wasn't a house. It was taller, sleeker; a coned apparatus. Just when the shape's spiral of blue and white ribbons came into focus, a white flash pierced her eyes. Sunlight glinted off the seemingly still-polished lenses at the top of the tower, despite its base being rusted by untold years of wind, waves, and sand. The lighthouse itself had refused to give up its luster even after what must have been decades of oxidation and corrosion. This worn oddity seemed bizarre even in a realm bare of common sense.

After a moment's awe, Lola traveled up the stairs that wound around the tower's height. Each step echoed as her feet clacked the metal in uneven rhythms. Halfway up, however, sound took its leave and slowly drifted out. Everything wavered away in distorted flickers. Suddenly, the stairs were no longer rusted, and the once age-ridden lighthouse dazzled as sunlight poured across its body. She normally would've been caught off guard at such dramatic change, but she kept on, unfazed, because this change was familiar. It resembled the warping scenery of the old wooden house.

Different structure. Same energy.

Different place. Same travel back in time.

An alluring sound played from the tower's uppermost floor, drawing her closer—"Hummingbird's Verse".

Waiting at the top was a circular room of glass filled with peach and pink-colored rays filtering through the panes. This time, the girl didn't appear flustered when Lola sat near her, softly, moving silently, as if noise would kill the ambiance making this room feel like a sacred alcove. Their eyes met in a calm blue coalition, undisturbed by each other's presence. They stared mutely at the vista offered to them by the height of the lighthouse tower, watching pastel clouds roll across the sky speckled with small flocks of petrels and albatrosses. Waves carried the whisper of velvet skirts. Breezes whirled with a salty aroma.

"You come here to escape your parents, don't you?"

The girl nodded simply.

"You know, I forgot what it's like being up here after all these years." Lola thought about spending eons here in this lighthouse, letting this warm body of metal and glass hold her in a secure, soothing embrace. However, staying here for long was impossible. The world would soon again dissolve back into reality.

"Why do we meet like this?" the girl asked.

Lola's composure softened. "Honestly, I hoped you might have some clues as to why this happens."

The girl looked confused.

"I've been talking with doctors about our, well, encounters," she continued. "They don't take me seriously, no one really does. No one knows how someone can talk to their past self or how a dream can be real." Her fingers knitted together. "All I get in return are pills—tons of pills—and sometimes a note saying things will turn out better."

"Ma won't believe me when I say you're real, and my pa just laughs."

Lola smiled, barely. "They were never ones for superstition, or whatever this is…"

"It's like we're dreaming," they said in unison, then awkwardly laughed. They existed in theory. For these precious moments, nothing mattered except their closeness and recognition of the other's hardship, a hardship that everyone else saw as merely fiction, something that was as real as fantasy.

"I was playing 'Hummingbird's Verse' again," the girl said. "Most of the time, Ma and Pa don't let me play it, so I sometimes come up here when they're not around to hear me."

Lola replied, "I've always been amazed that only you and Yercy ever knew about this old abandoned lighthouse. It's so far down the shoreline that hardly anyone steps foot here."

"That's why I like it."

"I know." She smiled more. "That's why I liked it too."

For a time, they talked nostalgically about what their lives were like, reminiscing over events in hopes of finding patterns, anything that could explain their story. To Lola, it felt strange hearing her younger self describe events that seemed so familiar yet utterly far away. And this wonderment worked in reverse. The girl was mystified upon hearing that, during her adolescent years, she would come to love and then sail boats across the summer ocean bays, watching fish swarm below the waves as Yercy tagged along, laughing. Perhaps it was dangerous revealing future endeavors, whether such memories were jovial or malicious in nature. Timelines had tendencies to meld or distort when brought together. That was Lola's theory, anyway.

Then the girl mentioned something peculiar, a detail previously overlooked. "You know, we've always played our song right before seeing each other."

"That's...true," Lola said, voice trailing off. "You were playing 'Hummingbird's Verse' last time I saw you. In our parents' house, remember?"

"Yes, when Pa punished me."

An awkward pause.

"Come to think of it, I was practicing 'Hummingbird's Verse' with my music teacher just half an hour before you showed up in my apartment." Lola stood, peering out the glass towards an ocean painted pastel blue. "It's a hunch, an absurd one at that, but could a song actually do this? I mean, it involves altering time just by playing a violin. This sounds straight from a fairy tale, but here we are."

The girl sighed. "And no one believes us!"

Lola sat beside her again. They were fatigued from unanswered questions. Their focus floated up towards the ceiling's metal surface, at oceanic silhouettes flowing across the canvas like cordial apparitions. One could simply rest here and admire the aquatic menagerie.

"I love music, though. I really do," the girl whispered. "'Hummingbird's Verse' is wonderful and playing it is also wonderful. But my hands…my hands won't let me play it sometimes. My hands feel really, really bad, and my tutor says complaining is pointless."

Lola turned to face her. "Perhaps there's something to my odd little notion about how this song brings us together." She cradled one of the girl's discolored hands in the same way one might hold a small bird. "Listen, I've been writing about our meetings in an effort to learn why this keeps happening, but I need more information. When will you be alone tomorrow?"

"Early morning, I think. Yercy and I love to play on the beach before my tutoring lessons. But the water's always chilly, so—"

"—so, we build sandcastles instead," Lola finished, remembering.

"Yeah, that's how it usually goes. Yercy's the only one my age who knows we're time travelers. She keeps telling her parents, but my parents make her parents scared, so none of the adults really talk now."

"Well," said Lola, "now you'll have another friend to spend time with." She felt the girl's hand squeeze around hers, not wanting her departure to be anytime soon. "I'll see you before too long. Just play our song when you're away from the house tomorrow, when your parents aren't looking."

Now, instead of worrying about the dreamworld crumbling or falling into vapidness, they were calm, lying there, watching the sky from afar until reality pulled them back once again.

Lola's body flickered.

Fading in, fading out.

And she was gone.

Back into the present.

Cyclical Misfortune

"… They knew not of the titan's origin, only that it rose leisurely from the east one autumn morning and eventually dipped under the western horizon, never turning back or retracing the path it laid behind across the soil…"

- Titan's Concert

Each word added to her journal slipped like snow dust from her mind and onto the paper. Mirror shards speckled the bathroom floor, the shower not used in days, and litter was strewn about the apartment. Times had plunged her into ruin lately. The most dreadful parts of her childhood had taken Lola by storm and blown her present life aside, bringing her to face what she'd wanted nothing more than to forget, forever.

I can't focus.

Can't think.

Can't sleep.

The night hadn't seen another hour in real time even though it had been much longer in retrospect. The feeling was akin to cognitive frostbite, a plight expanded to the point where she couldn't think without thinking of it first. Sleep would've been perfect, a calm to let her body rejuvenate from this trance. She was drained, deprived, forced to see through painful, heavy eyes refusing to close no matter how late it was. Restless agitation kept her tossing in the sheets, conscious of every minute passing by, slow, and slower, slower still.

What time is it?

Have I dozed off?

Morning came like a slow-breathing aura through the curtains. Lola didn't react even as it touched her face. She sat on the bed, staring off blankly. Everything appeared different, a muddled collection of objects bunched together without a focal point. Unseen, unrested, and unemployed, she second-guessed if this was real.

My head hurts.

I just need to wait longer.

Is this right?

Young Lola had a bedroom empty of toys and trinkets, save for the nursery rhyme books she'd open during the night's specter of haunted thoughts and memories. Her playground was the beach. Her only life-long companion was music. And the ocean waves never stopped; they whispered gently until she slept, until she dreamed of salt-scented air and Yercy's joy whenever a new sandcastle was built. The whole house echoed as if it were a seashell, reminding her that times could be held in splendor, cherished, like holding a brittle sand dollar.

If only such times lasted.

The girl's morning shower was cold this time. The hour fresh out of bed was often spent in solitude, knelt on the bathroom floor with a towel holding her body heat captive several minutes longer than if she'd stepped out naked. Those minutes were invaluable. There was a unique comfort in this small pocket of time, in this low tide of day when no one else had risen yet. Her guard could be down without punishment. Her attention could ease without facing a reprimand. Once her playtime outside was over, the day would change into a streak of routines vast with worry and hours upon hours…and even more hours still, of everything strict, rotten, and overbearing.

I must perform well.

...or else.

Evelyn appeared suddenly as the bathroom door flung open. She was dressed for someone who'd arrive hours from now and was wearing perfume laden with strawberries.

"Still naked and pathetic," the woman said. "A fully fledged outfit is required on days scheduled for longer practice sessions. You know the tutor has a scornful eye for unprepared clothes."

"Thanks for turning my hot water off, meanie," Lola whispered while her mother sifted through the hangers, standing obediently like a doll set to be fashioned by its owner, shivering.

Cold water down her back.

"Now this will surely impress," Evelyn chirped, holding a blonde-yellow sundress. "You'll be wearing this alongside a pair of white flats for today, understand?"

I hate that color, Lola thought, and her smile was plastic. "Yes Ma, understood."

"That's wonderful dear. Make sure you return home an hour early for some pre-session rehearsal. Your high octave hymns should be in top shape before today's rounds of training begin."

Although Lola remained at attention, her mind raced. The planned meeting with her big self had just been cut off. "Actually," she said in haste, "could I skip all that today? I wish to play by myself a little bit once Yercy leaves."

"To dabble with your new imaginary friend? Don't be childish, dear."

"But I am a child," she replied as if touching frigid steel, quick to withdraw. Their interactions normally functioned by clockwork agreements and docile compliance. There was hardly such a thing as contempt.

Evelyn glared—two knife-sharp emeralds. The girl's body stiffened, almost frozen beneath her spotlight. Her mother valued submission more than spoken apologies. Obeying often insured things would be painless.

"And I suggest telling Yercy about these longer practice sessions," her mother added. "You'll have more of them in the weeks to come, so they'll be less time to spend on less valuable activities."

The girl remained placid. *I get it. Less play time. The usual.*

Her mother left after ensuring the yellow dress was cleaned raw of its supposed imperfections. Instantly, Lola sprung from her chilled state and headed outside wearing her favorite royal blue sundress and flip flops two sizes too big. The doll-like persona could drop. Such things were pointless in a world free of pipe smoke and cheap fragrances. Finally, open air, open skies filled with laxity. A smooth birch walkway led towards the waves where freedom dwelled, and she said hello to the fine sand between her toes. However, Lola's attention was soon drawn into finding her best friend which, intriguingly enough, was akin to locating a precious jewel among the scenery.

Indeed, Yercy's appearance was a rarity unto itself, seemingly crafted from the shoreline's desire for stylized color palettes. Her eyes were filled with equal parts teal and fuchsia, and her hair was a clean mix of similar hues coming down in long streams. And in the early sun, her skin momentarily exposed its hidden shade of seashell pink. All their interactions were formed with mellow tranquility, as if Lola was actually speaking to the morning breeze itself, for they only met during those time when the tide was young and seabirds still slept. She of course knew Yercy wasn't human with her slightly webbed feet and pointed ears, and her skin that reflected a different hue sometimes. Her friend would have borne a striking human semblance, however, if all that color were to wash away.

"What do they call you?" she'd asked during one late-summer's dawn. "A ner...naieda...naeii...?"

"A nereid silly!" Yercy had replied, both of them laughing. "Or a naiad, or even a sea nymph. But I like Yercy more than any of those names, because it's my name and no one else's."

Whenever their paths crossed, they became guardians of sand-built kingdoms glistening wet against the young sunrise, sharing moments with starfish and hermit crabs watching peacefully beneath the current's face. In their beachside creations, cockles formed windows, sticks were bridges, and notions flowed like water through the inlet bays.

Lola spotted her friend now down the shoreline, a swathe of precious pastel. A half-built sandcastle waited by her feet.

"If we made a really big wall around this one, do you think it'll last 'til morning?" Yercy patted down another spire. "The urchins could sleep in it all night long and even watch the moon rise."

Lola scooted back, her flip flops squeaking. "They'll also need a doorway in case one wants to crawl out early, or if it gets hungry. What do urchins eat?"

"Plants, mostly plants I think, and sometimes an unlucky foot." Yercy laughed again and pointed seaward. "Hey, look out there! I see four sailboats all going in a row. That means good luck heading our way."

"They give luck? Since when?"

"Well, I was searching for flowers in our favorite basin, you know, near the old lighthouse. There weren't any around. Not even one." The colors in her eyes bloomed. "But when they came to pass—the sailboats I mean—a flower blew right on my nose. I almost fell back! Isn't that how luck starts? Lots of people talk about it. Good luck and bad luck, and luck in between. Or just luck." Hearing no reply, she turned back to find her companion's mood dissolved. Lola's eyes absently weighed down towards the sand.

The nereid sat beside her. At times, saying nothing spoke more words than not. Instead of galvanizing Lola with cheer or more stories about lucky sailboats, she wrapped an arm around her human counterpart, and they watched the first sandpiper scurry about in search of worms beneath the sediment. Morning aged as the ocean sparkled white—Strevenfall's late sunrise.

"Ma said to come in early for practice." Lola's voice hardly breached a whisper. "I don't know what to do. I promised my big self a meeting not far from now, but now we won't even have much playtime." She lay flat on the beach. "And I'm so tired, so *very* tired."

Yercy lay beside her, both staring up at cotton clouds and bird formations. "Our lighthouse is always a good hiding place. I won't tell anyone if you go there, promise."

"But I've never stayed there instead of going to a practice session."

"What about that crawl space under the docks?"

Lola shook her head.

"My parents' house?"

She shook her head again. "Ma would be so mad that I'll never go outside again. Or worse, she would take my violin away during play times. Then I would never see my big self again."

Yercy pouted. "I'm sorry, really sorry." She offered her best smile, not knowing what it felt like to have hands so fragile, like thin shards of glass, wounded, but kept a hair's width from breaking. The tutor knew exactly how much strain a little girl's bones could take before succumbing to overuse. A perfect recital held its weight in gold no matter the pain inflicted. If her fingers could retain their function and play, there was no need to fix them.

Once dawn grew old, the guardians departed from their kingdom, one heading towards a cottage farther down shore, the other towards a house where sewn bodies waited. But first, Lola played "Hummingbird's Verse" to call upon her likeness. The notes traveled on through history's otherwise frozen past...

...and into the present.

Like a wintry breeze, Lola felt crisp-chilled delirium take hold. The dream-filled ocean grasped her feet as the familiar specks on the horizon materialized before her eyes. Alongside the old, weathered home and rusted lighthouse, a sandbar stretched somewhere between them, adding to the abstract assortment of portals towards the past, and like the others, this one led somewhere different. This distorted realm bridging their

64

timelines had always been a mystery. She wondered if her younger self had ever stepped foot here, or if this place was unique to her experience alone.

Much like before, and as expected, static tumult spilled in when her feet touched the sediment, signaling the journey from the present to the past. When it lifted, the small patch of beach had opened up into a broad spanning shoreline speckled with shells. Waves whispered their oceanic melody, and in the distance a small blue wisp approached her, fast, running, desperate. Before Lola could react, the girl was hugging her waist, nuzzling her clothes.

"I'm sorry!"

"I don't understand. What happened?"

The girl peered up. "Ma's called me in early for practice. We can't play together now." She stepped back. "Yercy said I could hide, and she wouldn't tell, but I don't want to hide even if no one tells! I'll get punished really, really bad!"

Lola knelt while pushing away sleep's burden, for retaining what little energy remained was a constant affair. She looked towards the house that had been the birthplace of so many afflictions, then at the ocean, where tides flowed free of judgment.

"You look very tired. Please say something."

"Have you ever just…fought back?"

"What do you mean? Or course not. You should know that."

"But that's the problem." Lola clasped her shoulders. "I do know. I know exactly what's ahead if nothing changes! Years and years of torture. They'll keep making you go hungry. They'll keep the sunlight from you. They'll keep hurting you over and over again. You must understand that abuse isn't normal. You deserve better, especially from your own parents."

"Never thought about that, I guess." The girl paused. "What if Ma and Pa stop loving me?"

Lola couldn't help but laugh, hollowly. "This isn't love, trust me. It's a prison. As for me being tired, well, that's a new one, and unfortunately, it's getting worse by the day. I can hardly sleep no matter what I do."

A call echoed from the porch; an algid noise. Evelyn's chirp enveloped everything as her lavish attire flapped in the breeze.

"Oh, I have to go." The girl's tone flattened, laden with worry. She wordlessly headed off at a pace lost between acceptance and unsureness.

Lola watched. Their distance apart stretched like an imaginary tether binding them. Afar, her mother's eyes were spotlights that cared little for empathy or sandcastles built by shoreline architects who prayed for better.

Lola matched the girl's stride, moving beside her.

"What are you doing?"

"It'll be a while until my body gets whisked away again. I'm not letting you go in that house alone. For as long as I can change the past, I can help you."

"That's crazy!"

"I know. Maybe it's the lack of sleep."

The girl laughed. "Well, if that's so, please stay tired all the time!"

Their hearts grew still upon entering. Breathing was troubled when submerged under cheap fumes and tension. The house was a wooden shell turned into an hourglass whose grains fell half as fast. Evelyn went about like a fancily dressed peafowl gone aimless, setting up every precious picture and flower vase even though the shelves had been organized twice before.

Someone's wagon parked near the house outside, a discrete chariot pulled by two graphite-colored unicorns, the type whose appearances merged with the ocean backdrop. An emotion went off, Lola's brain flashing with a memory once hidden. She whispered to the girl, "Here, repeat what I say."

"Good idea, but you don't have to whisper, remember?"

Evelyn looked over, confused, but someone knocked on the door before she questioned her daughter.

The person who entered had dull gray hair with streaks of lackluster white, an unusual elf in that her features closely mimicked those of humans, save for the slightly pointed ears. Lola watched tentatively. The woman's eyes were silver, her clothes thin and wispy, like silk rags soaked with vapor, and she carried a suitcase in one slender hand, the other resting at her side.

It appeared, despite the woman not breaching thirty years, that she embodied some ominous spirit caught in clouded mystique. If all her muted shades were to bloom somewhat, she might have been beautiful.

"Please do come in and relax, Miss Valery." Evelyn's tone was that of a bird tweeting for its owner. "Perhaps tea would suffice while you unload?"

"I can do without tea. Perhaps later, thank you." Valery spoke with tainted layers, words veiled by covert intentions. She unbuckled the suitcase and rummaged through like a moth searching for dust, until her spotlights moved. "It appears you wish to say something."

The girl tried inching back, but Lola kept her steady.

"Don't be bashful. Speak up."

"Oh, well, I-I waded in the ocean too long. My fingers won't hold the strings very well if they all look like raisins." She raised her hands, smiling frankly. "See? Lots of wrinkles."

Valery raised a brow and knelt to inspect them, these intricate devices softened by the ocean, observing with impersonal scrutiny.

"We can settle for the piano this time," Lola said.

"We can settle for the piano this time," the girl said.

Valery glared at Evelyn. "Such is why I suggested play dates be cut short. Why wasn't my advice heeded?"

Evelyn's demeanor became strained. She uttered a soft, slavish-like apology, then left quietly.

"No matter the delay, let's not have our valuable time together be wasted on a piano lesson. That's not what I'm here for." She slipped off her thin taffeta gloves, two dark sets of fingers, and tossed them before the girl. "You'll be wearing these until I instruct you otherwise. Understand?"

The girl peered down, half expecting them to move like widow spiders. "They're a little big for me."

"Challenges are gateways to improvement." Valery took her spot, arms arched over the piano. "Every missed note yields one shock to the neck after practice, as always. Now let's begin. Start with the second nursery song you learned from last time and go from there. A tempo of around forty-eight would be nice."

"But Miss Valery, look. The gloves pretty much hang off my fingers."

No reply—an unbreakable barrier. Uncertainty crept in like cold woven threads up the girl's spine.

But just when they formed, a warm swathe slipped over her hands and made the tension ease. Lola's fingers splayed across her own like armor.

"Just relax, but not too much," she said. "I'll move the violin while you act in union. Remember, I'm not here."

Lola's snow-white dress kissed the girl's back like a cloak of alabaster. She could lean into it and feel the fabric's texture ease her muscles. The girl's legs were already somewhat spent after playing outside, but sitting down during these sessions was never allowed, nor was using the bathroom, or leaving the room at all, except when told differently.

So now, instead of the notes potentially being of poor quality, played by hampered hands, they sang out diamond clear. It was a relief not to panic at the whim of every song, not to just cope with the thought of getting through.

When the first song concluded, Valery wore an unreadable glare.

"I practiced outside yesterday," said Lola. "Works like a charm."

"I practiced outside yesterday," said the girl. "Works like a charm."

The tutor remained still—a plume of mist. "So, it appears, although miracles do occur no matter what."

"What? So perfect isn't good enough for you? Why don't *you* play this violin until your hands bleed!" Lola's nerves shivered. "Well go on! The suspense is killing me!"

The girl looked towards her counterpart's bloodshot eyes. "I...I just won't say that part," she whispered.

Another song ensued, this one a scale bouncing off with A-minor ascensions. It was played with clarity and crystallized design, a pure-as-glass gemstone bearing no cracks or nicks where conflict could form. Even with weary vision and diluted energy, Lola's every note was accurate, clean, spoken like a native language. Miracles didn't happen twice.

And yet the dust cloud remained stoic, hovering there with eyes never to see emotion permeate through them.

More hymns and songs came with each one's completion having near-flawless balance between pitch and rhythm. The instructed tempo of forty-eight never stepped above or below, nor did the sound breach unnecessary volume. Scales went by free of missed keys or strangled tones. The strings heated as the bow slid across them. Normally, completing this much material without errors was unheard of.

Lola bit her lip. "I don't understand," she said quietly, regarding how Valery's demeanor still hadn't changed, frozen to a mold. "Still, nothing? Why? Tell me the point of playing all these songs. The ceiling could cave in and you wouldn't even bother to look. You don't even blink."

Stillness echoed her soundless voice. She'd soon be left to meander through this mantra of exercises bearing no final verdict. It was just like before—reined into a state where following every instructor's command was the only way through.

"I don't understand," the girl said quietly, regarding how Valery's demeanor hadn't changed, frozen to a mold. "Still no praise. Why? Please tell me the point of playing all these songs. You don't even mention how much better they sound. You don't even blink."

Lola glanced down, surprised that she'd been mostly reiterated. Her last few remarks hadn't meant to be.

Valery turned back, facing the girl, her eyes flooding the room with palpable strain. With light movement she neared the girl and knelt before her. "Then perhaps you need a better look. Am I blinking now?"

No reply.

"A fragile tongue? Very well, then I'll ask you this. Why would someone like me have praise for someone like you?"

"Everyone should care," the girl said. "Do you care that I hurt a lot, all the time? Each poke with that shocking thing makes me feel worse. Sometimes I can feel it during the night. I wake up sometimes and I can't move, and it hurts."

"Your answer, child, while honest, doesn't reach far." Valery returned to the piano, as if her next words needed space for momentum. "Perhaps you need clarification. Even If I were to end the regimen and actually care for you, do you think the situation would change? You are merely a speck in an industry of thousands. Understand? What prodigy would want to go about their days knowing that? So many people practice music, child, yet only some have achieved your talent." She paused. "When you train with me, I'm actively changing all that. I can make you known to even the greatest arenas with hundreds of eager eyes. You will become known across the realm of Strevenfall. Loneliness and strife will just be concepts long since forgotten. It doesn't matter how much it hurts, or how much you whine in the short term. You just need the courage to see this through."

The mental echo of her words came in swells, slowly, churning in Lola's mind. The girl replied, "Yes ma'am," as if being sullied was fair game. The session resumed because speaking out against the instructor's staunch idealism would only lead to more pressure. If Lola was being cynically honest, she'd consider if bringing about change now was two steps away from absurd. She could ease the pain, not the outcome. If there were other options left, they remained hidden.

The girl's fingers tensed like wires in a piano. She stole a glance up to see her older self's complexion drained into dismal unease, frantic; someone who had nothing left to say except the dolesome truth.

"Please, you have to stop shaking," the girl whispered. "Such things aren't allowed. If you do it, I'm likely to follow."

"Then follow!" Lola snapped. "Neither of us will change anything if we don't show the heartache she's causing!" She hurried around in front of the child and knelt, obstructing Valery with her reddened sleepless eyes. "Listen, I'll be fading away again any minute now. You have to say something to change Valery—anything—or else it'll be years until this finally stops." Her body flickered, her face, her hands. Having no words left and no more seconds to spare, Lola embraced her counterpart gently, taking in her faint shoreline scent.

The girl watched her older self dissipate in static ripples flickering from the room, leaving nothing left save for a sudden quiet absence. She felt exposed, left in the tutor's shadow. What could dispel it? Emotion was fruitless, as were pleas, and every form of contempt had been laid bare.

A threat?

A threat? The girl withdrew from the thought. Yet, what else could she do?

Time flowed onward. Lola was reeled from the past and deposited once again into the present.

Waiting for the next call of "Hummingbird's Verse" this time had her thinking of nothing else. The tension in her head and in the air had reached a point where going back was beyond comprehension. She was emotionally splattered, each feeling strewn about her apartment. Resentment was limp near the corner, with melancholy stuck on the ceiling, and over there, hanging from the bedpost, was loathing. Perhaps an eviction notice was tacked on her door outside. Maybe Garenham University had one less student in its roster. Meanwhile, it wouldn't surprise her if Sandy's Diner had already replaced its absent worker. She'd sacrificed dearly for this, a dream that no one else could see and few could understand.

It came again—finally—that familiar static flowing through the space in her mind, taking her back to the strange amorphic land bordering the two timelines. Yet something felt amiss upon arrival. The ocean was silent, stagnant, drained of even the wave's whisper in her ears. The current had seemingly lost its voice.

A too-bright glimmer fluttered in her eyes. It came from the lighthouse; somebody within its glass-enclosed top floor. The glinting halo beckoned her across the water, soundless, but something seemed to pull back as she second-guessed her actions, the inner world's last subconscious warning before it could no longer reach its tired wanderer. Worried and weary, she followed her feet towards it, towards the only light left in view. There was a shadow stitched to her heels that tugged against every step through the endless ocean. Had her actions during the previous visit altered time beyond repair?

Where have I gone?

What have I done?

But surely, this course of action remained the only way now.

The old lighthouse steps flickered away when she reached the summit. Velvet-peach light poured in around two figures, not one. Yercy stood near a window, flashing light off a broken windowpane. Nearby, her young counterpart sat idly in the center, not meeting her eyes, hands buried in the skirt of her dress.

Lola stepped forth, softly uttering a hello, as if speaking louder would undo the strange tightness she'd felt after entering. She uttered again, louder this time, but just as soft.

The girl hardly moved. "You can stop making signals, Yercy. I can see her. She's here."

Yercy stopped and looked around, though her sight phased blankly through Lola approaching her counterpart ever so slightly. "Where is she? How close?" The nereid's expression was that of post-traumatic grief, her mouth straight. "I'm really scared. Are you going to tell her everything?"

The girl nodded. "She's there."

Lola knelt, leaning in, but the girl winced and jerked away. Had simple eye contact caused her pain? "I can tell you're hurting," she said. "What happened?"

"What's going on?" Yercy stepped closer upon seeing her friend's reaction, then backed away, not knowing which was best.

"I didn't know what else to do," the girl mumbled, blinking away tears. "Maybe showing what I've done isn't such a good idea. What's the point? It's over now. No more sessions. No more teachers."

"Show me what? Are you hiding something? This is…" Lola's voice faltered. There was a dark red splotch on the girl's dress, spreading slowly. She looked back up. "What…what happened?"

The girl hitched on a breath and revealed her hands.

The sight stunned her to the core. Lacerations covered her hands, bleeding down her fingers and palms, and the crimson glass piece lying nearby indicated that the injuries weren't caused by another. Her hands had been voluntarily and deliberately maimed by dragging the jagged glass across them again and again. The skin was shredded and had ulcerated sores. Infection had already begun to take hold.

"I-I couldn't think of anything to say, except a threat," the girl said, voice cracking. "But threats to the teacher wouldn't do anything. So, I threatened to hurt myself instead." Tears rolled down her face now and she stared at her self-inflicted wounds, wounds that were deep and grotesque, wounds that were disfiguring and had started to fester.

Lola snapped out of her shock-induced trance and scrambled for words—begging her younger self for forgiveness. But her pleas had no effect as the child's adrenaline had faded. The pain and realization of what she had done struck her like a hailstorm.

"No one believed me when I threatened to do this!" She was screaming, sobbing. "And now I'm here! I did it! I showed them! Now they can't use my hands!"

Horrified, Yercy tried soothing her companion out of her state of panic, but her focus fell out of tune when she noticed that her own clothes were now stained with someone else's blood.

"Big Lola!" Yercy cried. "If you're out there, please help her! Please!"

But Lola hadn't any means of correcting what she'd done, the lighthouse chamber swarmed with cries filling her head and body. Her sense of control was gone, yet still she tried quelling the bleeding that threatened to leave her child self unconscious on the hard metal floor, or worse. She ripped ivory pieces from her dress and knotted them tight around the girl's hands, staining the fabric, soaking it.

Footsteps echoed from the stairs below, sounds drawing closer in on the uppermost floor leaving little time to prepare. Frantic voices churned like unshapely songs spelling an end to secrecy. The lighthouse had been discovered by outsiders, it was no longer a solace and shelter for the girls.

Evelyn appeared from the staircase, heels clacking, face twisted with appallment. Calvik followed behind, his expression mimicking hers. Then the elven dust cloud parted their shoulders and stepped in front. Valery observed the scene with something between surprise and disappointment. The girl was already feeling distant, meanwhile, her vision blurred from suddenly weak limbs and a shallow heartbeat.

"Don't look at her like that!" Yercy stepped forward, eyes wide with fury. "You did this! You all did this! Just go away! This is *our* lighthouse!"

"Go home Yercy!" Evelyn's tone cut right through the nereid, and she pushed forward with each of her footfalls ringing through the floor and sending high-pitched echoes across the air. The nereid tried fending off this intruder only to have Calvik hold her aside, his hands rigid. Evelyn was on the verge of grabbing her daughter to scold her, another reprimand, another dose of punishment.

"Stay away!" Lola tried to shove her mother. Hard. Hard enough to hurt her. Hard enough to hopefully scare her into believing an angry ghost wanted her gone from this storybook hideout made from metal and glass.

But then, the world unwound. Just when her hands made contact with Evelyn's skin, she was stopped by a force beyond comprehension as her nerves locked with ice-cold pain. Everything and everyone had paused, and it felt as though the air pressure had suddenly risen, reality caught in one frame of time, crackling and popping. Lola suffered to find a reason for the change as her mind raced from one thought to another, until it clicked with terrible weight.

I touched someone.

I've touched someone in the past.

I've touched someone in the past, besides myself.

I've touched someone in the past, besides myself, or my child self.

I've never done so before.

A huge noise fractured the space like a violin string snapped from its fingerboard. It pierced her ears as static waves tore apart the room's shape and color so viciously that she felt nauseous.

Everything was a motionless image, ruined by razor-sharp distortions. The lighthouse rippled away as something pulled her forwards in time, towards the present, forcefully and without compromise, without warning.

I've touched someone...

The force was deafening.

...in the past...

Violent.

...besides myself...

Agonizing.

...or my child self...

Then there was nothing, her body floating in the silent dark.

Deafening. Violent. Agonizing.

She awoke in the living room of her apartment, cloaked in the same ivory dress now ripped and sullied with blood stains. Her pulse raced near its limit like a hammer beating in her body, until she was left folded on the floor, sweating, heart pounding. She eventually managed to stand but couldn't cry for help. Her lungs were spent as if she'd just ran through a snowstorm. Nothing in the medicine cabinet held answers; just a broken mirror with Dr. Hane's pills strewn about. She sat against the wall, clenching her chest, wading through cold spells without patterns to speak of.

Slowly, the pounding softened and eased as it spiraled down. When it finally settled to a normal rhythm, a chilling conclusion weighed heavily on her mind, one made clear by her drained limbs and blood-stained dress.

The dire truth was that, throughout this entire ordeal, she'd unknowingly caused far more harm than good.

Dream Machines

"As such, Talvren's surface was a cybernetic landscape of circuits that glowed neon red as data traveled through them. The oceans were large bodies of energetic plasma. The sun was an artificial heat source controlled by a room-sized grid."

- Yeal

Lola bore a heavy mind made from iron and feet filled with lead, for they were firmly planted, held hostage by the ground. She'd hung onto a corrosive goal threatening to rust her down. She'd wanted to cling to the past but came back bearing stiff breaths and burdensome thoughts. She'd unknowingly made a timeline worse than what it was before, guilty of every taken chance to make her childhood different.

Now unsettled by more than two days' lack of sleep, she walked like an ungainly robot, stiff and tired. The blood-stained dress, evidence of her crime, had been replaced with a clean, copper-colored shirt and pants. It almost felt refreshing to wear something new like this. She stepped carefully among the glass shards strewn across her bathroom floor. She'd tried cleaning them up only to find that doing so through tear-soaked vision was an accident in the making. Several hours had gone by since being ricocheted back to present times. Most of them had been spent dealing with nausea spells aching her head and stomach, all the while feeling like she'd swallowed a gallon's worth of something fierce. By now, the pain in her head was familiar, but the stomachache was something new. Thankfully, it seemed to be improving and perhaps passing out of her system.

Resting a spell had granted her a little more energy, at least. Proper deep sleep still remained the only means of recouping what stamina she'd drained thus far, but now it seemed more akin to an unattainable pleasantry. A mental wall veiled her mind whenever she tried moving from shallow rest to anything beyond. Her brain operated like an aged set of gears, worn yet working enough that she could at least think of a better option, the next step. The journal entries in her bedroom—she looked them over, scanning each line, then added to their testament everything that had transpired since her last writing. New details were coming clear and connecting. Rules seemed to exist that governed every journey into the past timeline. She made a short list of a few in particular that stood out:

- My younger self and I have the ability to send each other to our respective timelines through the song, "Hummingbird's Verse".
  For example, if my younger self plays all or most of "Hummingbird's Verse", I am transported into her timeline shortly after. This effect also works in reverse.
- I am unable to calculate how much time passes between transfers. I only know that, after a short while, I am pulled back into my original timeline by an unknown force. This concept likely works for my younger self as well.
- During the transfer, the only one who can see or hear the other 'self' is the one who played "Hummingbird's Verse". We can still physically alter the world, however, like moving objects around. This practically makes us ghosts of some sort, at least temporarily.

Aware of all these mechanics, her brain resonated with the question of, *where to from here?* These unseen laws didn't seem malleable, but most laws were prone to loopholes, and could be exploited. Going forward with the same methods of dealing with this ordeal would result in the further deterioration of her well-being. Something had to change.

Suddenly, an idea came to mind.

The violin had been exiled to the dresser's bottom drawer. The motion of lifting it out was only vaguely familiar. She held the instrument as if it were paper thin, picking up on recent memories welded to its body. Simply playing "Hummingbird's Verse" again wouldn't resolve or improve anything of substance. The transfer process required a new design, for the girl's sake. Lola rummaged through her bedroom storage trunk, sifting through old metronomes and pitch pipes until a brass glint caught her eye. It was a device akin to an old gramophone, only much smaller. Yercy had offered it as a birthday present some six years ago before she'd moved out alone.

"Here, it's to keep track of all your favorite songs," Yercy had said.

"Thank you, thank you so much," Lola had replied, the gift cradled in her hands. "I'll make good use of it, promise."

She blew a thick layer of dust from its many grooves and notches. The small contraption had both a microphone and a tape player in one compact chassis. Household audio recorders had been marvels several years ago. Strevenfall's collective knowledge and collaborations had brought them into the music space. Prior to that, radios once held the pinnacle of progress.

After adjusting the mic head towards her strings, she flicked the power button on, paused for a moment, and then assembled "Hummingbird's Verse" from line one. Lighter than lithium, each note played with worry for their potential misshapen sounds. It was just a matter of convincing them that perfection wasn't necessary. Soon, page four was complete, then five, then more. Her arms operated on tight hinges as they cycled through the sounds, until the song finally finished.

A faint disturbance murmured nearby. Light from outside trickled upon the girl who'd materialized close to an open window. Bandages gloved her hands while a patient's gown clothed her body. They met beneath the bright aura of noon, their hearts heavy and their eyes filled with concern.

"Your clothes, your bandages. Who's taking care of you?" Lola questioned.

"I'm in a hospital right now, a great big fancy building with lots of rooms. They just wrapped me up and said to sleep for now." The girl looked at her palms awhile. "My room's pretty much empty except for the nurses who come in sometimes. Yercy hasn't visited me yet. Maybe she can't. I call her name but another someone walks in instead of her."

"Sleep…Were you sleeping when the transfer occurred?"

"Transfer?"

"When you lifted away from that room and ended up here."

"Oh, not in a million years. My hands still hurt way too much for dreamland. My muscle tissue is severely damaged. It may be infected beyond normal scarring. That's what I hear people say, more or less. It's really dark in that room except for lots of small lights that beep once a while. My parents are also nowhere in sight. Ma's likely furious."

In theory, those words should have inclined more of a reaction from Lola, but she leaned back and breathed tiredly instead.

"You look awful," the girl whispered. "Well, I don't mean that kind of awful, just, you look rather empty. Please don't get mad."

"I'm not mad, but I am a basket case, to put it bluntly." Lola held the child's wrapped hands. They were covered in multiple layers of gauze, rendering the girl's fingers and hands nearly inflexible. Upon closer inspection, she noticed small splotches of red peeking through the outer covering. "Don't worry about me, though. Once you leave me again, just concentrate on getting well. Agreed?"

"Yes ma'am, I guess."

"Good. That's good. Here's what's been going on. Lately, I've started compiling a notebook, a testament of sorts describing our meetings, recording important details, what causes our time travels, things of that nature. It's my hope that by doing so, I can figure out this whole mess. Suffice to say, this isn't something that happens to most people."

"Oh, you mean like a dream journal?"

"Never really thought of it that way, but yes, I suppose it's a dream journal." Lola knelt so that their eyes were level. "And I need your help filling in the blanks."

They gathered around the coffee table just as noon faded to eve. The girl had first dibs on any stray pillows or blankets. They took turns reciting key events about their melodically induced time travels. Lola's spirits weakened as she filled line after line, page after page, with her younger self's harrowing tales of physical and mental misery that included Calvik's brutality, Evelyn's condescension, and Valery's cruelty.

It wasn't long before memories covered the paper, some well remembered, others chaotic and foreign. A radio nearby debated with itself as two voices crackled back and forth about recent happenings. The girl had at first been startled by the small box holding a thousand different sounds, then had been mesmerized, realizing this unfamiliar world had many strange devices, each one speaking their own electric language.

"Ma's radio looks really big compared to yours. How do they fit so many people in there?" The girl's question faded as she noticed that her counterpart had grown still. "Hey, are you alright?"

"It's almost cruel making you say these events out loud just to get your side of things." Lola flipped a page. "Reading back over them, some are the stuff of nightmares."

"But we're almost done, right? Just one more bit left?"

Lola inked the feather quill and held it above the next blank page. Her hand was shaking as she struggled to focus—to stay awake.

"I could try to write the next part, even though I...can't. You look so tired."

"No, it's fine, I think. Now, we're up to our last meeting in the lighthouse. This took place several hours after we separated during Valery's session, so let's start with what took place between then and when I climbed the stairs of the lighthouse and saw you." Lola glanced at the bandages. "What happened?"

The girl pulled her blankets up. "Yes, well…"

For a while, only the radio spoke, which somehow thickened the silence that lingered between them now.

"It's fine. I'm here. Just take your time."

"Right. So…when you disappeared, I stayed with Miss Valery for a tiny bit longer. She wanted to punish me again. I tried to push her away, but nothing worked—then I had this idea. If Miss Valery was so interested in my hands, what if my hands were not able to hold anything anymore? I yelled and escaped out the door with my violin. I didn't look back. Then I ran to get Yercy, and we headed for our lighthouse much farther down the shore. We were sure no one in the whole realm knew about it except us."

Lola glanced up. "No one saw you two go up there?"

She shook her head. "You know all those glass pieces on the top floor of our lighthouse?"

"I do."

"Well, I knew they would be very sharp—sharp enough for what I planned to do, but when I told Yercy about my idea, she tried stopping me." The girl's body tensed as if the blanket had turned to steel. "I yelled at her to back away, yelling loud, like grown-ups do sometimes. After that, I found a really sharp glass piece, took a deep breath, and dragged it as hard as possible across my hands…"

The next few phrases caused Lola's hand to shake even more as her mind instinctively tried blocking out her counterpart's voice, but she forced herself to listen. Some letters jabbed through the paper. After the silence turned awkward, she apologized, tore away the page, and copied it to the next one, but her face had yet to lift.

"A-and that's when you came to help me!" the girl added suddenly. "You ripped pieces from your own beautiful white dress and tied them around my hands. One doctor even said that, 'Without these timely wrappings young lady, things would've definitely been worse.' And another nice lady nurse gave me a fun book to read, since I can still turn the pages. Her name's Kaitlyn. I like her. She even said there's a playing area downstairs from my hospital room."

Lola stared at her now with a new, unreadable expression.

The girl was confused. "What? What's that look for?"

"How did you do that?"

"Do what?"

"That. What you just did."

"What did I do? I don't understand."

"You!" Lola proclaimed. "After all that's been said about one of the most dreadful parts of our lives, you've still managed to find a friend and something fun to do." She started laughing, not knowing or caring where it came from or where it was going. "Look at us! We're a mess! Yet somehow, you've shown me a reason to feel a little less down about this whole ordeal." She leaned back. "Or perhaps, I've finally gone mad."

"I don't think you're mad. Because if I'm you and you're mad, I'm also mad, and I don't think either of us are mad."

Lola's smile grew after hearing such playful logic make more sense than anything else had in a while. Resting her quill, she brought out a very peculiar-looking machine from beneath the table. Bronze sunlight reflected off its many faces.

"What's that thing? It looks kinda odd."

"Just a little something I got for you." She placed the recorder between them and flicked the power button. "Hummingbird's Verse" sung with frictionless tones, crackled only by the speaker's age-old mouth.

"Lovely…" The girl was transfixed, engrossed. "I've never heard our song being played that way before. Everything's so clean." Her body relaxed to the progression, the steel blanket softening. "Honestly, I didn't know our song could even sound like that. I bet this took a whopping ton of practice. I can only imagine."

This was indeed a first—the girl hearing her counterpart's take of the song in person. It made Lola's surprise ease into something fainter yet relaxing. "Whenever the need strikes," she said, "just press this button here. If my judgment's right, I should be sent to your time within minutes."

"Wait, so you're not sure if this'll work?"

Lola shook her head; a silent apology.

"Then what if I do it and nothing happens? Nothing will happen, that's what!" The girl pouted. "That'll be really, really bad."

"It's all we have right now. Believe me, if I'd come up with a better idea, we wouldn't be doing this."

And so, their respective farewells came across as only somewhat assured, neither one fully confident if the unseen laws accepted loopholes or bent rules.

"Goodbye for now—I hope," the girl said as her body flickered, before fading completely.

Much to their relief, the recorder's speaker played, and time responded. After crossing the strange realm between, Lola was brought into a small room illuminated by an old lamp resting on the nightstand. The walls were even slates of beige marked with graphs and pictograms showing mostly body parts. On the ceiling, a shoreline painting coated the surface in wisp-like colors, an attempt at comfort for when nights grew stark. This place was a sleeping creature of silent machines who'd swallowed a child, all while having a fake semblance of somewhere nicer.

The girl waved her over. "We must be really careful. People come in here every now and then. Most of them stay for just a little bit, but others do all sorts of things with their odd-looking toys, and that takes longer."

Lola propped herself against the bedside, finally able to breathe off some of the weight collected in her thoughts. Whenever someone entered, she backed off—five steps away at least—making sure not to touch them, keeping out of reach. A rule she'd recently added to the journal list made it clear that physical contact with anyone other than her younger self resulted in a forceful reset to the present that was both mind numbing and horrendously painful.

A pattern made itself clear once the second doctor left—a shift in their expressions, their cadences, their collective character. The hospital staff showed kind gestures when turned towards her younger self, but turned away, those expressions flattened, plated with concern. Most were young or in prime, so it wasn't as if they'd been hardened to an act after decades of good-willed service.

Stepping around the constantly moving bodies prompted all sorts of risky maneuvers that forced Lola to a near-constant waltz along the tiles. Three steps back. Two steps forward. Half a swerve left. Spin like this. One two, one two. The girl stifled a laugh whenever she'd performed a new creative dance sequence in efforts to avoid contact. Having a performer's swift feet offered an unexpected aid with all her movements. More withheld faces showed signs of something wrong, meanwhile. She needed answers.

Lola finally spotted a gap where she could escape the room without causing any ghost-like commotion. A doctor had swung the door wide, and it was closing back slow enough to pass through undetected.

"Where are you going?" the girl asked, gesturing in confusion.

"Stepping out in hopes to find something," Lola replied in haste. "I'll be back shortly."

She kept near the doctor's pace and followed her through carved-out channels of carpet entwining like a circuit board, all the while keeping a mental anchor on the girl's room. Avoiding passersby proved an unwieldy game where the player sidestepped collisions along narrow paths. Open windows revealed a small townscape where birches lined the roads instead of palm trees. This building stood so far from Strevenfall's shoreline that hardly a trace of it showed.

The hallway ended as Lola followed the doctor into a pale murmuring room where several more white coats gathered. Before them were notes and schematics depicting foreign shapes. She ventured closer, one foot advancing, the other held back, ready for a split-moment's reaction. Strange tension accumulated whenever someone's voice stopped and others began, as if everyone here had simultaneously witnessed the ceiling crack open, but no one dared to mention it.

"I'd give this scenario three months, four if treatment goes well." An older man with silver-white hair, perhaps the hospital's administrator, spoke in a soft, steady voice. "Until then, our job is to make her comfortable. Any objections?"

"Do we tell her?" someone asked.

"No," he decided, after a tense pause. "It'll ruin her if we tell someone that young. We'll make certain our patient receives company from those she's closest to. Every day counts infinitely more now. Keep that in mind."

"Tell us what?" Lola went unheard.

When they departed, she accidentally brushed someone's garments with her arm, but thankfully skinless contact didn't seem to induce a reset. The room was empty now. Colorless lights above gave shadows their darkest contrast. Everything was either pale white or midnight black, a filter where hues couldn't thrive. People's notes were left arrayed along the table, stacked neatly. While no one else was watching, she gently closed the room's door, waited a moment, then hurried over to review them. She scanned the piles, finally settling on one labeled 'conclusion paper'. On a whim, she stopped to read a passage which indicated that matters had deteriorated far more than she thought. Her eyes dropped down to the small closing statement far below its preceding text.

Her breath hitched upon reading it. She set the pile back and stepped away, feeling flimsy, unstable, her balance wavering as the truth buried in her mind, little by little, each second heavier and heavier. She slowed her thoughts, not able—or not willing—to process the writing all at once; the doctor's dreadful verdict.

"Oh no," she whispered tightly.

Lola stepped into the girl's room, sat against the back wall, and then stared blankly at the floor, her shaking hands balled into fists. The girl didn't even notice her re-entry until the door finally clicked shut. Their eyes met, a silent bridge arched between them, yet nothing crossed from or to the other, one pair of sapphires confused, the other empty.

Lola moved to rest beside her counterpart in bed, gingerly cradling the girl to her chest and repeating the words, "I'm sorry, I'm so sorry", each time softer, until her voice trailed into nothing but a whisper.

The girl peered up nervously. "Sorry for what? Did you get in trouble?"

She bypassed the question using cordial gestures, tucking her in, asking if she was comfortable—a caretaker's checklist. It made the girl's expression waver, its foundation set to give. What was that face looking down at her? Was it happy? Solemn? Or caught somewhere between?

Grown-ups are strange.

Back in the present, the doctor's verdict came down in one definite sweep over Lola's thoughts until nothing remained but her own worry. She'd jotted the closing statement down on a piece of paper while in the meeting room, having also swiped a pen in the process. She took that paper out of her pocket now, reading the words once again.

...Our peer-reviewed investigation has confirmed that the pathogen found in patient 229's (Lola Jay Pern) hands matches that of the Kronitare virus, an infectious agent prevalent along the Fervine coast, which was where the patient was exposed due to self-inflicted wounds on the fingers, wrists and palms, using a contaminated glass piece located in the area...

Peering out the windows towards Garenham's evening townscape, her mind repeated the statement over and over again like a broken vinyl disc.

...Because of the time elapsed between the incident and her arrival at our hospital, we caught the virus in its more advanced state, one in which its effects

can only be delayed, not corrected. Based on recent studies of Kronitare, we expect the disease will continue spreading throughout the patient's hand muscle tissue, breaking it down, ultimately resulting in severe loss of motor control in those areas...

Lying restless in bed, she kept lacing her fingers tighter and tighter. Her mind was stuck on repeat, still broken, near frozen with the fear she could no longer ignore, the dread she could only hope would be worse than reality.

...The virus is projected to render the patient's hands useless within the next three months, though we may be able to extend that time if treatment goes well. From there, we will have to consider more long-term applications to help prevent the disease from infecting more regions of the patient's body, especially her vital organs. Amputation of both hands and/or a permanent schedule of antiviral drugs may be required. If we do not stop the virus's spread in time, the effects will lead to death, which in this particular case, unfortunately, seems the most likely outcome.

Her head felt like concrete by the time morning rose again. Another mere scrap's worth of sleep made the truth nearly impossible to bear. She ran through what happened, sorting out the familiar and the unknown, writing it down, reading it over, recapping, recollecting.

Lola suddenly stopped after realizing how fruitless her train of thought was becoming, almost snapping the quill in half.

I can't waste time, she thought. *I can't waste anything.*

Staying still would only eat away the minutes now that every day was precious. From here on, she had to build each waking hour from scratch so that not one second was squandered, condensing the space between her actions. She had three months, four at the most. That was ninety days to save her younger half. Ninety days starting now. Starting right now.

The main library was among Garenham's most prized possessions, a mostly stained-glass body framed with smooth oak beams, twenty-two floors bound by corkscrew stairs, enough square feet to swallow an entire plaza. Inside was a world unto itself. Painted light embellished the bookcases and tables. Gizmos, from three-dimensional astronomy maps to hand-crafted realm globes, lined the end caps, like punctuation marks to eons-long sentences. Lamplights saw little use except during overcasts and at nightfall. She skimmed the book spines on the uppermost floors in search of records with the keywords, 'Kronitare' and 'beach-native viruses', or some variation of the two. What was left of her focus, eroded due to being starved of sleep, was allocated towards this one task, this one goal. Those who walked near or engaged in conversation were passively ignored.

Lola arrived at a standalone table near a window, holding three medical publications whose page counts spanned well into the hundreds, if not more. Pages turned along with the clock. As time progressed and the sunlight slipped away, it became obvious as to why doctors hadn't designed a widespread cure for this Kronitare virus. Accounts on it were elusive even with present-day technology, over ten years later. Small bits regarding the virus were sparsely littered among countless paragraphs filled with useless data, useless to her at least. Her patience wore thin.

She went back for a second look through the isles, never giving heed towards outside affairs, only the task, only working towards what mattered. She may have been an android lady created to examine a small-sized parameter. She paused only long enough to reconsider her approach, that perhaps locating data on such an unheard virus demanded a more centralized approach, rather than devoting focus across many sources that yielded little information to begin with.

She pulled out a Fervine coastal realm directory and flipped to the medical listings. Fervine was the small strip of beach where she'd spent her childhood. Only two were mentioned, one named 'Fervine Hospital' and a second called 'Medical Research Bay #44'. She chose the second, and over the following days investigated this bay #44's procedures, social funding, its staff members, and more. She eventually came across a testimony by an elf named Rustem Kavlador, someone whose record piqued her interest. The book in which she found his name had been lying near the bottom of a corner shelf. Although it appeared quite old, its publication date indicated that the text was fairly recent, being printed no more than three years ago.

Her focus sharpened as she read the book's closing remark.

...My concluding statement is as follows: There lies an underground basin at the foot of Strevenfall's northernmost region, within a cavern likely carved by a former subterranean river. The water there is saturated with a family of minerals that, based on my previous studies and from testimonies given by the locals, all of which are mentioned above, appear to have properties that could reverse the same type of muscle degeneration effects found in the Kronitare virus. Kronitare, named after the now-destroyed moon of Strevenfall. This mineral water would likely not completely eliminate the virus's effects alone, but with the aid of other stimulants common among the health field in general, it might be a great candidate in ridding the realm of the Kronitare virus...

Those words stuck to the back of her mind as if they'd been soldered there. This discovery was like an answered prayer, lustrous in her thoughts, causing her heart to leap. After recording Dr. Kavlador's report into her dream journal, Lola went home to draw out the coordinates around Strevenfall's northern region on her own personal map. Sure enough, a place called Stalactite Cove was found. She marked it. All of her research had merged together at last, a cure for an illness considered terminal in the past, but correctable in the present. She'd found a way to save her counterpart's life.

She studied the map, drawing a line from Garenham to Stalactite Cove, a path going through Fervine's coast, her childhood home, and on through Strevenfall's more exotic terrain.

She spent the following night making laps around her apartment, sorting her thoughts, her arms crossed below her chest, coming up with the same realization every time. She needed to put her plan into motion. Her past self's condition spelled an uncertain fate for her in the present. Would she herself perish? Would the future be erased because of her attempts at changing the past?

There was no better choice now except to leave. No doctor or medical institution would order this rare mineral water, and no one would ever believe her haphazard case, at least not here.

Traveling throughout Strevenfall would be dangerous with her muddled sleep cycle. She needed help.

Only one person came to mind, a notion like waves rolling softly within her emotions, someone whose name brought memories made of oceanic tides, of pastel remedies; a companion for the upcoming voyage.

She wrote a letter when morningtide rose and the sun had churned through its early hours. Explaining her recent trials and tribulations, she asked her childhood friend for the favor of her companionship across Strevenfall's landscapes. This person had been the subject of her thoughts several times throughout the years, ever since life had caused them to separate. With any luck, their amity still held firm.

Waterbot

"Who said the clock tower couldn't be scaled? I sure didn't."

- Glave Octus

Two days after mailing the letter off, Lola arranged for her departure. She packed in preparation; several days worth of clothes, hygiene articles, any remaining currency, the dream journal, and navigation tools for when the route became perilous, all bare components for a prolonged journey across the realm. Her violin and partly filled suitcase were well within the train station's weight capacity rules for long-distance wanderlust. After cleaning up the apartment, it was off to Garenham University and Sandy's Diner, where she would finally explain her absence. Whether they believed it to be a contrived fairy tale or not, she needed to completely resolve any loose ends and ultimately detach herself from this part of Strevenfall entirely.

Mr. Krayble nodded, cupping her shoulder. "I'll try postponing your last few exams indefinitely. Best wishes in sorting things out."

Iris was at first frustrated, then understanding. "You're leaving for now? Okay...well...fine. Don't worry too much about it." She placed a hand on her shoulder. "There's always an open spot for you here."

A whistle howled over the train station's scenery of steam, metal, and late-morning shine. Her carrot-orange sundress hardly stood out as other brightly clothed pedestrians bustled about. Among her favorite aspects of living here was that no matter how industrialized the architecture became, the city's engineers always knew to keep nature's style up front. Strevenfall obviously didn't overlook putting color here where the railroads briefly joined with Garenham's outer city. The lampposts and flower bushes glowed against this smooth ambiance as they led along the walkways towards the paying office; a mostly glass dome with alloy latticework holding it together. Tickets covering the kinds of distances as what she'd planned held cumbersome price tags. Paying for this train ride had already chiseled away at her budget. Being careful was a must. At least the train would be peaceful as few were heading where she was.

"All aboard!" called a green-suited man, waving his light.

The train whistled once more as its gears rumbled to life, moving slowly at first before gaining speed, the engine acting like a metal heart pumping heat through its many pipeline veins. It was like rain to Lola's ears, a tempered sound easing through the seat cushions and kindly up her body. Her focus could withdraw and take residence somewhere between her thoughts. Five other passengers had booked the transit coastward and they were sparsely scattered about the car. Those who sat in couples sometimes muttered among themselves, adding to the soft, synthetic rain.

She allowed her focus to seep beyond her window and look out across the world as it raced by. What began as a city, dense with paved roads and stained-glass buildings, was becoming a countryside vista speckled by old oak houses and stores. Orange and gold lights flurried by in the form of glinting blurs, nudging her away from existence to where her drowsiness didn't need to be fought with. Fervine's coast was a childhood land her eyes hadn't touched since she was a teenager. With any luck, it was still that mystic stretch of beach curving up to where the land touched seawater; a timeless venue.

Not long into the transit, flickering static came upon her like television snow, falling in to fill the space with crackling intensity. Soon, she was once again wading through that bizarre pocket dimension separating past from present. However, this time, instead of water, she was trudging through a sea of oil, which tugged down her steps like wet pavement. Air infused with hydrogen sulfide galled her nose and throat as her eyes welled up from the fumes. A lighted match would have kindled everything in seconds. Massive gears floated high above, spinning slowly amid the rust-colored sky. It was a strange world teeming with floating metal and octane. Further along, steely pillars silently watched from where the lighthouse once stood, platinum columns that were overwhelming in size, unknown to reason. Why were these here? Did they matter?

There was also a different structure—not her parents' house—a building positioned quietly in place of where it once sat. She roamed through its hushed empty rooms and staircases in search of something other than hollowed space, or perhaps meaning behind this suddenly changed dreamworld. On the top floor waited a room whose inside was completely taken up by pure, perfect blackness, a vague mass that stopped right at the doorway's threshold. Static flickering scrambled her senses again as she ventured within arm's reach of it, sending her back towards the past where her younger self had been indefinitely bedridden. Now, Lola stood calmly by the little girl's bedside as she slept there. Nestled between her arms was the recording device she'd given her not long ago, the one that enclosed "Hummingbird's Verse", keeping the song just one button away.

Must've pressed play on accident.

A question formed when Lola awakened back in present times, back in the belly of the train. The dream realm had abruptly changed. Why? She wrote the question in her journal and studied it. The obscure gutted building from the first leg of her most recent trip shared semblance with the hospital the girl was staying at now. Surely, they were connected, but how? There had to be something that explained how, or why, the trips were

94

at first mimicking a clear blue ocean and then now taking the form of some abstract wasteland of oil with cryptic metal structures.

The train's progress was interrupted occasionally as it stopped to let aboard passengers from towns closer to the shore. Each group who boarded wore garments that were progressively more and more embodying oceanic styles—loose-fitting and sleeveless, embracing coastal palettes of wispy silk and light cotton. By that evening, outrageous colors formed a kaleidoscope inside the rail car. Her eyes slipped from body to body as if to photograph their outfits and store them away. Missing the quiet of the near-empty carriage from hours before, Lola started frequently visiting the caboose to enjoy the open scenery, watching the fleeting vista of hills steadily slip away as they dissolved into brackish marshland.

A passing log cabin reminded her of when she used to visit abandoned cottages miles out from Fervine. She would play songs to feel how they echoed, her violin's language drifting through the rooms like vibrations in a shell. She would also venture beyond the town's outer lands in search of untouched, abandoned buildings, drawn in by rumors of hauntings spun by townsfolk. Homes made of old rotting materials would muddle the notes while newer homes tightened them.

Years prior to that, she remembered swimming in the amber pools along Fervine's easternmost region, where the water had undergone complete discoloration from various natural chemicals. Or was it bacteria? She'd always stayed long after nightfall to watch these pools come alive as they all discharged their tiger-orange light, radiating like huge bioluminescent organisms. Diving below the surface would reveal a world where one could float limply among the soft aquatic glowscape.

Lola traced her memory even further back in time, when imagination fueled life and escapism was always the answer to the harsh, unforgiving mechanisms of reality, in a time that seemed like it wasn't a part of her life anymore, fragile moments mostly faded out by the years. Among these memories were images of her child self joyfully practicing with her first violin. It had been a birthday present gifted from a local instrument shop.

Evelyn and Calvik were much happier then, before that interest in music evolved into a talent, then a dream, and that dream was abused into a nightmare.

It was a world deficient of background waves absorbing the hushed night hours. The girl lifted from sleep more than once, expecting anything but her room's impartial silence. A life mostly spent on shore had accustomed her ears to the shoreline's hymn, no matter where she stood, or what time. Time? What time was it?

"What time is it?" the girl asked.

No one answered.

Lying awake in darkness for this long had built up an odd relationship with her surroundings. She could pull under the covers, roll around, and hide under a pillow, all while blind to her movements. The room wasn't a room, but a formless black expanse where light had gone extinct. She lay on the soft floating island of sheets and blankets with many hours' worth of unspent energy. Assigning play names to objects made for a good distraction, but games like this were silly if there wasn't foresight into how long they would last. True enough, boredom and time were symbiotic.

Morning's only presage came as footsteps muttering through the walls, then as voices, then as light splaying across the room when a nurse knocked twice before stepping in, typically a young woman carrying fresh rags, gauze wrappings and scissors. These daily treatments were the unique occasion where her hands breathed fresh air, when their dense outer shells were peeled off for maintenance. Those who entered the girl's geometric world worked nimbly around her swollen scabs. Touching the bare wounds flared pain across her fingers. Dialogue was rarely exchanged. And what was behind those strange looks they gave her? Their eyes acted curiously whenever a pair swiveled her way.

"What do you think, Tinman Tom?" she asked the recording device, who'd been given the name overnight. "Everyone acts like a robot. Maybe it's because they're really far from the beach. Being away from the ocean can make anyone act strange, perhaps." Her eyes drifted around. "Listen, we should go exploring. Bedman Berry can guard our room while we're away."

The room's size expanded when she slid off Berry's side and touched the cool tiled floor. Cracking the door open revealed a tunnel of sallow walls and windows looking out to a place miles from the shoreline's embrace. Thankfully, no one was near enough to see her step out into the pallid hallway. She held Tinman Tom tight, feeling its warm metal, yet her arms nonetheless shivered.

Then she peered back towards her room tag.

The label read, *Hospice terminal care room #71.*

Shadows greeted her back in the room, along with a certain dread that hadn't yet clicked into place. Terminal was a word that remained like a timer fastened to her body, deadly if allowed to reach zero. It almost didn't register, but the tingling rivets pricking up her spine proved that she knew full well what the label meant. Grown-ups always shared dire faces when 'terminal' laced their dialogue, so why wouldn't the people here do likewise? Why were they silent, seemingly calm, their voice boxes muted?

Bedman Berry's height far exceeded her ability to make the climb back up its side, so she took refuge by curling up underneath, wishing that these past few minutes had merely been a dream. Imagination was such a good place to hide.

A Wishing Well in a Land of Disbelief

"There is no such thing as an absolute dogma."

— Miesu; sage of the moonlit waters

Morning dawned on the watercolor land where every breeze sang along with the wind chimes that many hung from their porches and patios. The air carried like a whisper between the scattered houses, and as Lola left the train station, she caught a whiff of brackish nostalgia in her nose. She had arrived during Fervine's most delicate hours when low tide exposed the coast to reveal its hidden shell treasury, mobile homes for bare-backed crustaceans.

She didn't need a compass or map to navigate the sand-strewn trails. She remembered well the paths that wove among the buildings and parks, like strings stitching the landscape together. Her first stop was the open food market, then a sun hat store, before coming upon Fervine's beach where the whole town of thinly placed cabins and shops could fill the view; scattered shapes whose edges softened under a blush-pink sun, all like a muted painting. How long would it take before all the line work dissolved? Everywhere she looked was once a safe harbor of her childhood, when days moved slow enough that morning and evening seemed bound to a slow waltz about the sky, that same ageless sky in which she used to count stars

98

and pick out made-up constellations shaped like music keys. Now, she walked while the waves sometimes reached far enough to kiss her feet, as if to remind her of those very moments encased in honest sentiment.

High above the water, glass-winged swallows and cloud-scaled serpents watched her search for one building in particular, one capped by a periwinkle roof and a chimney puffing up rings of walnut smoke. It was both a repair shop for those who had broken hulls or torn sails, and a womb for what the locals called wave gliders—small sailboats stylized with soft effortless designs. If her memory proved true, it would still be just a few hundred feet back from the berms, situated evenly between two palm trees, the same ones where a small flock of birds lived that would always pick at tourists' lunch baskets if they'd been carelessly left ajar.

"There you are," Lola remarked upon catching sight of the shop. She continued along the narrow path leading up to its back door that, to her pleasant surprise, had still kept its shell-shaped knob after all this time. She went around front rather than unexpectedly barging in from the back, where light coming through the stained-glass windows enveloped her body. *"After all this while,"* the building might have said, *"you've returned at last."*

The inside was that of a nautilus's inner spiral, walls covered in airbrushed pictures of schooner ships, wispy shades of hues that all coalesced around the person moving behind the front desk. Lola's dearest companion had always appeared born to dwell among a coastal town such as this, and now, after seven long years of absence, it was like coming upon a breathtaking yet familiar jewel stone.

"Look who it is!" Yercy's powder-blue dress fluttered as she embraced Lola. "You took faster than I expected getting here. Hopefully the shop wasn't a chore to find."

"Not too hard, and you still use that shell-shaped knob you made when we were kids," Lola said. "That was part of your homemade tiara at one point, wasn't it?"

"Once upon a time, yes."

They stepped back from their embrace but remained holding hands as each looked the other over. Yercy's complexion embodied a pastel dream; fair, almost opalescent skin, pointed fish-finned ears, and long hair that shifted from seafoam green to cyan, depending on the light, and was streaked with magenta. And of course, those eyes which held the colors of watermelon and mint. There was nothing harsh or sudden about her complexion, as if the ocean itself had painted it, giving it life and movement and feeling. Her figure hadn't a single straight outline, choosing instead to blend together as one whimsical form, and she spoke as if every word deserved its own supple appeal, a voice brimming with elysian charm.

"Does Fervine still look good on me?'

"Like it was always meant to be," said Lola.

Yercy chuckled. "What about my species name? You always have a hard time getting it down. Come on. Let's hear it. I bet you can't."

"Oh easy. You, Miss Yercy Rivitine, are a subclass of elven nymphs known as a nereid. Nereids can hold their breath for up to twenty minutes, are great swimmers, and require more skin maintenance on days over eighty-one degrees. Basically forty percent elf, forty percent human, and twenty percent mermaid."

"Whoa, you got it down, and then some."

"About the only use for Garenham's ecology course—random trivia." Lola paused. "I left not a day after sending you the message about what's been happening recently. Time isn't really on my side."

Yercy nodded sensibly. "I got the message yesterday. We…we should definitely talk about it. My cabin's farther down shore near the docking bays. I can just slip out of here with a note."

Lola smirked at this. "You mean the sailor, Brishon, still owns this shop? Only he'd let that slide."

"Yep. Things may have changed, but not terribly much."

While heading out, they passed through a storage room holding rows of newly made wave glider parts—rudders, tillers, hulls—all disassembled and ready to be connected as working bodies. Here, a vessel's individual style depended heavily on the shipwright's imagination, molded from raw wood and canvas into instruments that could skate along the ocean's face, drawn forward by coastal winds. Leading the way, Yercy walked with a demeanor so fluid one might mistake that she was sliding along the floor, or perhaps the floor was instead moving her.

Why can't I be that calm?

Lola remembered when Yercy had finalized her love for boating by adopting this trade. They were both sixteen when the paper arrived confirming her employment into the lifestyle she'd always yearned to embrace. Lola herself would have likely joined her companion in this dream, this aspiration, but their paths had diverged, and she'd only been a month away from her freshman year at Garenham.

The cabin's inside was that of a seafarer's retreat, pinewood rooms festooned with model ships and giant sea creature paintings. Cool drafts made the otherwise humid atmosphere welcoming as they sat at the porch table upstairs, their skin coated in soft vanilla light. Above them, turquoise chimes danced together to sing about peaceful times. A seaside view always turned difficult conversations into something brighter.

Yercy held the letter. "From what I've read, you're waist deep in quite a dire mess. This paper reads like a curse. How many people know?"

"Only a few," said Lola. "My doctor, a friend at work, and my music instructor, but I think they see my dilemma as a bit too bizarre."

"Fabled up?"

"Yes, fabled up. I mean, who would take my case seriously? Time travel is unheard of even in the magecraft scene."

"Well, *I* believe you."

She sighed. "That's a relief. You're really the most important one I wanted to hear that from. Other people seem to have me confused with a crackpot."

"Which brings us to your letter's other subject. Your wobbly sleeping habits make traveling alone quite tottering and tedious."

"Tottering?'

"It means unstable. Sorry, my ocean-speak has taken up my vocabulary." Yercy's eyes softened as she turned away, stretching, loosening the next phrase in her mind before speaking. "The letter asked for some company while you journey to Stalactite Cove, where this allusive cure for the Kronitare virus is."

Lola nodded.

"I would have to drop everything and leave for a whole month, maybe two."

She nodded again.

"And Strevenfall gets pretty varied where you're heading—valleys, forests, basins. Whatever can't be traveled by boat or horse carriage will be on foot. Not easy at all." Yercy leaned back, regarding the horizon. "But from a different view, this could be my excuse to get away from mundane happenings and see what landscapes are out there."

"This is a tall favor, I know."

"When are you leaving?"

"Preferably tomorrow."

Yercy moved back inside to wander like driftwood in the living room, arms swaying aimlessly, staring at the ceiling as if to plaster her thoughts there and sort them out.

"On the fence?" Lola asked.

"This all came out of nowhere," said Yercy. "Your offer could be enchanting, or dangerous, or both. And yet, who am I to say no? If I said no, you could wind up worse off than before, wayfaring while severely sleep-deprived." She leaned lazily against the back wall. "I don't know, Lola. I really wished we'd reconnected after all these years under different terms, you know? We haven't even talked, let alone visited each other since you left for Garenham a long while back. This decision's gonna be an overnighter. Let me parse things out, alright?"

"No one can force you. I understand if you need to think—" Lola was interrupted by a sudden static-filled vertigo and she staggered back.

"What's wrong?"

"I-I think it's…"

Lola fainted. Yercy barely had time to soften the fall as they both stumbled to the floor, her collapsed and unconscious companion on top of her. Wincing, she awkwardly carried the body upstairs where a small candlelit bedroom would ensure its safety until the owner returned. Indeed, Lola's time traveling took place exclusively in the mind, not the physical self.

"Sure picked a lousy time to visit the past again." Yercy stepped up slowly and gingerly. "Good thing you didn't hit any furniture."

A few white coats were knelt around the hospital bed like seagulls drawn to a capsized boat. Lola performed an outlandish sequence of pivots and curves to maneuver around them, following their eyes underneath the boat where "Hummingbird's Verse" was finishing up its last few notes.

"Please come out," pleaded one doctor. "We can help you."

"What's that music?" asked another.

The little girl's complexion had partly lost its color, matching more with the faded sheets of her bed. On all fours, Lola shuffled closer until she could drape an arm over her younger self, as if to provide shelter in case the bed collapsed. Outside, a worried face often dipped low enough to capture them through the darkened gloom, holding them still, before lifting back up to converse among the rest.

"Make them go away," the girl said.

Lola had no response, bothered by the statement in question, because it wasn't a question. It was a command so innocently stated yet so distant, withered even.

"Please make them all go away. I tried and no one listened. Those dummies."

"What happened?"

"These people can't help me. Never ever. Not one."

"Nonsense. Why say that? You were happy a few days ago. Remember? You talked about how there's a playroom downstairs, and about someone named Kaitlyn who's very kind. And also…" Lola's mouth hung open mid-sentence, her next breath contracting as if she'd suddenly been caught in a bind.

No. No, not yet! I must be certain.

"My question remains," Lola said. "Please, tell me what happened."

Nothing.

"Please say something. Little good comes from hiding under a bed where people can't help you…I'll listen. I promise."

The girl covered her face. "I don't want to, alright! Just go find my room name!"

The words were abrasive, but Lola wouldn't let them hurt her, and she wouldn't let her counterpart dissolve into dread.

"Hey, hey look at me."

The girl did so, eyes dampened.

"Listen to me. I'll find your cure."

"Huh?"

"Yes. In fact, I already know what the cure is. It's just a matter of getting to it. There's knowledge in my time that simply doesn't exist in yours, understand? In my time, the cure has been found, or at least documented…" She went on to clarify the nature of the Kronitare virus in simple terms, before revealing that a mystical place called Stalactite Cove held a special mineral water that could undo its effects. Each phrase permeated through the girl's ears to rejuvenate the lively spirit in her eyes, her paleness somewhat receding.

"Where is Stalactite Cove?"

"Far," Lola answered, and noticed that the girl remained doleful. "Not too far, though. Close enough that I can remedy your virus before time runs out."

"How much time until it runs out?"

She revoked her first reply before speaking, choosing a vague one instead. "Not long, but not too soon. Enough time. Just place as much trust in these doctors as you do in me. Everything else will be fine. Understand?"

The girl gave an almost imperceptible nod.

Lola nudged her on. "Now let's get out from under this bed, unless you actually enjoy being cooped up down here."

The tiny giggle she received meant that she was doing something right; a profound relief worthy of its own name.

On the nightstand, a cyan candle splashed light across Lola's face as she awoke to an empty room. Downstairs was equally vacant, no one else home, just the wall paintings and other baubles that made the house into an inner world, its owner's stylized taste dwelling freely throughout the area.

A delicate rustle carried her eyes to where the dream journal sat opened on the porch table outside. Its pages flapped over as if a ghost was turning them.

Minutes later, Yercy entered the home carrying large produce baskets loaded with bright exotic fruits and plants and set them on the table. They appeared like ornaments as she sorted them out, all in a manner so easy yet so utterly fixed. When their eyes met, however, she still personified an aura that could never be fixed, as if being fixed was an act she merely called upon whenever circumstances permitted it, never letting the act take over. It was only a tool, a plaything.

"A family could live weeks off of this," Lola said. Stating a simple fact now was better than making assumptions.

Yercy replied, "Or two people for two months. Fruit hardly stays ripe farther down shore where the marshlands are. It's best we get our food here before leaving. My sailboats at the shop can hold plenty more than what I have right now, so there's extra room for clothes and other items we might need." She flicked up an ornament and caught it. "We'll ride about eighty feet from land where the current's nice and steady. That'll keep us in a good spot between traveling ships and those who may be out swimming near the beach."

"That's…" Lola almost found the urge to object, put off by her friend's sudden change yet fascinated by how natural and jubilant it sounded. "I-I'm very glad to hear that, quite honestly, really…*really* glad. But are you ready? What about this house? Payments can't fill themselves. And what about your sailboat shop?"

"Oh, well, physical do-dads aren't worth their price in clam shells compared to what we're soon embarking on. I already let Brishon know that I'll be gone awhile. I also have quite a heavy sum in savings."

"My journal's on the porch table."

"I read it through and through."

"Believed every word?"

"Every single word, front to back."

"And…how convincing was it?"

"Oh, horribly convincing." Yercy's expression flowed into what might have been kind acknowledgment to what the journal described, or simply a modest nod. Her mood softened any emotion that would've been clear otherwise, all wrapped in some halcyon-like countenance guided by its own temperament. Relaxed. She was just relaxed. It was fascinating. "Though," she went on, "my mind was nearly set when you blacked out on me earlier."

"Oh," said Lola, and she grinned modestly. "That bit was also rather convincing, wasn't it?"

"Pretty much. I mean, who'd really make a better traveling acquaintance besides me? I'm the only one crazy enough to believe in your supposed fairy tale."

Lola's expression brightened, her grin widening. "Thank you."

Yercy found herself caught in Lola's cobalt eyes, baffled, mesmerized.

They awoke during low tide, when the morning was young and dawn had just crested over the warm sand freckled with shells. The sailboat shop was empty during these hours, so they could pick out their chosen wave gliders, load their hulls with supplies, and bring them onto shore by way of horse carriage. It was decided that wearing light clothes over bathing suits would be best for countering sunburn, all while keeping cool under the shadeless coast. Lola wore a sleeveless, sapphire-blue top and white shorts. Yercy's top was light purple, matched with green shorts. Sun hats and sandals for both.

Yercy nimbly adjusted her vessel's rudder and tiller, and afterwards tied the sails, all as if assembling a large toy. Wave gliders appeared dwarf-like compared to normal sailboats, sized only for one passenger and not much else besides cargo, but their simplicity meant fewer malfunctions and lesser trouble steering. They headed north where Fervine's shore turned white with quartz sand, the township giving way to bare beach and scattered islets. Lola was surprised she could still operate a wave glider by muscle memory alone. It was an instinct that had remained clean, regardless of time.

Waiting ahead was a grand enclave covered in umbrella trees and rock formations cloaked with moss. Upon its beach were old cabins strewn like the skeletal remains of bodies, all tangled in vines splaying across their frayed wooden skins and worn foundations.

Yercy noticed her friend's reaction. "Recognize them? It's been a while since you've gone this far up the coast."

"Our childhood homes," said Lola absently.

They pulled into shore and approached the cabin straight ahead. The entry door moaned an unpleasant greeting when Lola pushed it open. Inside was a time capsule made from ramshackle wood and rooms partly filled with morass water. It was the house where Calvik and Evelyn had once raised their daughter by means far beyond rational discipline. With Yercy following, she waded into the living room where sea kelp hung over a crumbled fireplace flanked by two rocking chairs.

"Mother always looked through the performance letters Valery issued after practice sessions." Her voice had dwindled now, as if speaking louder would extol too much emphasis on happenings that deserved none. "Of course, low marks meant a night downstairs away from our candles, where the temperature dropped to match the night. That punishment was always given during the winter. As for summer and spring, it was the attic."

Yercy watched her hand trace along a table, watched her face become weighted with a somber, almost vacant countenance.

"I remember them sitting here, right here where I am, talking endlessly about Valery's reports, nothing else. My plate would either have little food or be empty depending on those reports, those damn senseless reports. After dinner, Mother sentenced me to other punishments if grades averaged lower than the previous session—days kept in the large closet upstairs without windows, or perhaps…" Lola stopped, forcing distance between her words and emotions, pointing a line going about the room. "They would have me go naked until Valery returned again, no matter what I did, often while doing chores outside."

As they plodded further through the bog-like rooms, Yercy remained voiceless. She knew that what her companion needed now was a listener, not a commentator—a gentle pair of ears to absorb the dialogue, not someone who remarked on delicate events.

They neared a doorway sitting at the end of the moss-covered hall. Lola opened it warily, like a hushed apology towards her already bitter thoughts. Light cascaded through a ceiling hole and into the room where dolls floated like the corpses of shipwrecked victims. Their bodies were mostly decomposed by years of water, yet all their eyes were open, lifelessly awake.

"Solo exercises always took place here. The dolls had been Valery's idea, I guess as part of her deranged fetish." Lola appeared like she would have continued. A rancid, washed-out feeling caused her to sit against the back wall, blankly watching the dolls float about in the pool that now submerged more of her body, yet she didn't seem to care. It was a silent mockery, a place that had seen countless shock therapies and despair had eroded into a brackish quagmire, as if the house itself never cared for what happened, never caring about Calvik's inert face when he'd pressed the electrocution device against her abdomen, while the dolls peered down like an audience caught in a sterile trance. It didn't even have the courtesy to deteriorate where she could no longer see it.

Only after leaving the shore and riding out at sea again did Yercy ask how she was feeling.

Lola replied, "I wish that place had been swept away entirely."

The lighthouse stood above the foliage not so far away, watching them depart from its land once again.

Drawn With Coastlines

"Strevenfall has the greatest population of pirates in the known universe as well as the greatest spans of ocean. If you want adventure, simply travel out to sea until the water turns dark."

- Cecil; commander of Merbull's naval fleet

Fervine's ocean was a liquid mirror poured between the islets. They've seen four days thus far, seafaring north where the tides leveled and the waves flattened into glass rippled only by their motion across its surface. Lola imagined herself caught among two pieces of sky, a world spreading out from the horizon as perfectly equal halves, coexisting, leaving gravity and gravity alone to decide which way was down.

There was a ludic quality to Yercy's presence as they sailed. She was like the ocean's expressive impulse given mind and body, the humble extension of its form that was her very being, and as such, seemed incapable of judgment or ridicule, displaying only a calm happiness of all things existence had to offer. It was a breathing energy, conscious of the way it moved and communicated through her actions, as if merely being there was enough to satisfy its purpose.

During nightfall, they'd often lay on the wave gliders themselves and doze off, unconcerned about waves or swells that would otherwise capsize an unsuspecting craft. Only an anchor was necessary. It was like sleeping in a bath of fireflies. The sea perfectly mimicked the clear night sky. Lola made ripples with one hardly submerged finger moving in circles, watching how the liquefied stars changed shape, tiredly amused, but stopped when she looked across the water. Yercy lay in her own glider nearby, wide awake.

"You mentioned something peculiar before heading off some days ago." Lola's sentence frayed into a question near the end, unsure if 'peculiar' matched this context, or if another world satisfied it.

"Did I?" asked Yercy.

"Yes. You mentioned how physical things aren't worth much compared to what we're doing."

"Oh, I remember now."

"Isn't that peculiar, though? It was as if the idea of leaving your home and shop behind came offhandedly, almost without a second thought. In fact, the only part you ensured safety towards was the job itself, the employment, something not so physical at all, the savings notwithstanding." She paused, then continued hastily. "Now, I'm not being ungrateful. I really, truly *am* glad for the company. I simply can't help but to think I've placed you in a bad spot."

Yercy's features livened, the effortless flow of her lips and eyes so gradual that Lola felt suspended in a trance, as if glancing off might cause some unspoken tragedy.

"I'm sorry."

"Sorry for what?"

"For sounding ungrateful. Questioning your choice now is ridiculous."

"No, not ungrateful," Yercy said. "It's an important question, though it's not really a question you want answered, right? You were just curious."

Lola nodded.

"Here, imagine a light bulb floating between us."

"What? Is that really necessary?"

111

The nereid laughed.

Lola imagined—a floating thought shaped into a glass firefly.

"But wait, instead of electricity, this magic light bulb is filled with purplish-blue water, and it glows mysteriously from within."

Lola reshaped her thoughts—a magic bulb.

"The purplish-blue water bubbles, then evaporates into a mist, revealing a smaller light bulb inside the larger one. While our larger bulb still glows mysteriously, this new and smaller one within it glows yellow, like normal—two in total, each glowing a different color. With me?"

"I think so."

"Alright, now repeat my game until you imagine one too many light bulbs. When that happens, just imagine all of them exploding in one loud noise." After a short while Yercy asked, "How many?"

"Well, four."

"See? We formed magic light bulbs, played a game, and caused them to explode using only our thoughts as materials, rather than actual materials. My idea for this game was inspired when I strolled by a store counter with bottled ships on it. A bit random maybe, but so is inspiration."

Lola raised a brow. "So our game proved that your reasoning isn't so crazy after all?"

"Still crazy, perhaps," Yercy replied softly. "Who would know?"

Dawn rose as they neared an isle curious from the rest, a small flat piece of land without vegetation elevated just above sea level; an ivory disk. The isle was first made visible by its only possession, a shipwrecked galley protruding straight out from the sand, half buried, nose up.

Yercy wanted to explore what was left of the bigger boat, so she parked her wave glider while Lola napped on hers down shore. Sleep durations lasted roughly five hours when left undisturbed, followed by seven waking hours. This cycle eased the gulf between night and day as her time was spent equally under the presence of both. It brought a new awareness of their slow, silent whirl above the ocean where night and day flowed in one never-ending streak of movement.

Awake now, she checked the time and recorded it.

"So, I won't actually see your child self," Yercy said, "only a ghost."

Lola nodded. "A ghost to anyone but me. My timeline and hers exist independently, isolated from one another. Like ghosts, however, we can affect each other's world—moving objects around, throwing stuff, anything physical."

"But not people, right?" Yercy read from the dream journal. "'If either of us make tactile contact with anyone besides ourselves, we are forcefully sent back into our original timeline. This occurrence follows up with very painful symptoms.'"

"Yes. It's like having two streams placed side by side, with one person swimming in either. Both can hop into the other's stream and splash around, but the streams themselves never cross."

Lola raised her violin and played "Hummingbird's Verse". Notes flew. Sounds fluttered. Soon, she saw her younger self cloaked in hospital wear.

Yercy saw disembodied footprints and knelt gently. "Hey, Lola from the other stream. Recognize me?"

The girl nodded, smiling shyly.

"She does," Lola said. "Also remember that only I can hear her speak. Guess it makes me a translator between you two."

"Then let me start off by saying it's a pleasure to speak with the youngest time traveler in Strevenfall's history." Yercy moved closer to the footprints. "How does it feel?"

Lola translated. "She says it's freaky, but Tinman Tom and Bedman Berry have been keeping her company when no one's around, and when people *are* around, they're put off by her new sleeping habits. Doctors just don't know what to think of her."

"Tom and Berry? I almost forgot that you would name your favorite knickknacks and whatnot whenever you felt the need. I remember our sandcastles years ago having some pretty outlandish names, like Sandbrook James, or Crabface Cenary."

"And we even named the crabs and urchins we found to put in them, though most never stayed for long," the girl said, looking off. "Where are we?"

"And we even named the crabs and urchins we found to put in them, though most never stayed for long," Lola repeated, then unrolled her map across the sand and pointed somewhere between Fervine's main coast and the grand forests further upland. It was a zone shattered into fragments of land dotting the old paper like dust grains.

The girl smiled. "Never seen this part of the realm before. It looks funny."

"Because most never bother to draw up maps for these parts," said Lola. "Even on stilts, homes are nearly impossible to build where the land is so unpredictable. Some islands vanish during high tide. We're having to sleep on our gliders in case the ocean sneaks up on us overnight."

"Did you learn these information tidbits from Garenham?" asked Yercy.

"More from personal research outside of class. Still, it took weeks to find my own map—tore it from a tattered almanac likely older than all three of us combined. We're pretty much treading on foreign grounds here, but it's the shortest way to Stalactite Cove."

"Still better than my hospital room. People always look at me strangely there." The girl paused. "Hey, ask Yercy if she still likes building sandcastles. We could make a huge one with a beach like this."

Yercy noticed Lola's reaction. "What did she say?"

"Well, she wants to build a sandcastle."

The day warmed into its afternoon glaze as their creation took shape near the shoreline, a smooth fortress made for crabs and urchins to find comfort in, sprinkled with shell fragments, glittering against the sky's deepening orange canopy. In a small celebration, Lola played a simple tune balanced on three chords, then played it again with added melody keys, and again using more note variations, each iteration more intricate than its predecessor, a song wielding flats and minors interwoven within a four-line motif.

"You play differently compared to our younger years," said Yercy. "It sounds better, or however musicians call it."

"Cleaner, is what my instructors say. Though it's easy playing around friends. Mr. Krayble, one of my instructors, would have students play before his class of roughly two hundred."

The girl's eyes widened. "That's a whole bunch of people."

"Mr. Krayble was mentioned in your journal," said Yercy.

Lola nodded. "Yes, about how my first time traveling symptoms came during a practice session with him. I was playing 'Hummingbird's Verse' in hopes of correcting the tremolo near the song's halfway point. I've always had a difficult time playing that tremolo, but nothing compared to the visions during my visit with him."

"Do you think his session caused what happened to you next?" asked Yercy. "I mean, when little Lola first showed up in your apartment."

"I don't know. Why would stress alone have caused anything? Or did I have to play 'Hummingbird's Verse' while being in a stressful position? I can draw conclusions as to how our time traveling works, but doing so fails in explaining how it all began." She leaned back and sighed, letting her hair fall; a curtain of ink. "On top of everything, I still know little about the space separating our timelines, that strange dreamworld."

A warm dusk had settled in, marigold waves lapping softly at the isle's beach where Lola and Yercy watched the ocean grow dimmer, its light slipping under the far-off horizon. The girl had left hours ago.

Lola let her thoughts flow. *If the dreamworld exists separate from my timeline, could I ever figure it out? And if it's not a part of my younger self's timeline as well, could either of us figure it out?*

They departed the next morning, heading through vast spans of ocean dotted with coral reefs stretching miles long, fathoms wide. During Lola's sleeping periods, Yercy dived down and explored the underwater cities where marine life schooled among pastel spires and sponges.

In the other timeline, morning had reached its brightest hour when young Yercy visited Fervine Hospital, and the girls' features livened with joy as they played among the pale delicate rays flowing like water into her room. Adult Lola watched how their interactions moved as one unified string mostly made from silly jokes and games, yet there seemed to be a weight holding it back. Her younger self hardly laughed. Yercy laughed too hard.

Yercy's father, Brimothy, was a wiry elven nereid with waves of soft white hair and eyes of the purest jade green. He stood at the doorway, watching them calmly—knowing the importance of their time together but all too aware of its approaching end. Nurses circulated in and out, checking on the girl's bandages while asking if anything was needed. Lola was glad she'd become adept at the art of dancing out of everyone's path.

Large bright lights and marble made the downstairs lounge an achromatic expanse filled with harsh outlines and shadows darkened by contrast, yet it offered more room than the floors above. Little Lola and Yercy found a plethora of games to play there despite lacking the ocean's sandbox.

"So, what's this doohickey for?" Yercy pointed at her friend's strange bronze box.

"My time machine is named Tinman Tom," the girl said, "and when Tom plays 'Hummingbird's Verse', he sends me into the future, or a *different* future, I think. It was a present from the other me since my hands, well, my hands..." She raised them, ivory mittens blending with the background.

Yercy's hands covered gently over her friend's as if they would crumble upon anything but the barest touch, then led young Lola to a corner obscured to most eyes, her own eyes glossy.

"Why are you sad?" the girl asked.

"Why? Why are you *not* sad? Daddy said you have something very dangerous, a disease." Her voice thinned. "Lots and lots of diseases are

116

cured, but this one is different. This one might not go away, and if it doesn't…"

"I'll be alright."

"No, you don't understand!" cried Yercy. "If your disease doesn't go away, *you'll* go away! Forever!"

When the girl explained, it sounded more like a fictional narrative than one pulled from reality, but Yercy listened as if fiction had been reality all along. Her composure returned, equally holding the qualities of being intrigued and mystified.

"So, Tinman Tom is from the future, and the cure can be found," the nereid mused, then paused with a look of question aimed towards her companion. "What's wrong?"

"My hands are hurting again. Must be time for medicine soon."

"What kind of medicine?"

"Well, not really medicine. Someone comes by to change my bandages and clean my hands with a special rag, so the stitches won't peel off. But maybe they shouldn't even do that. The pain feels worse, and sometimes my fingers get fatter, you know, like what happens after a wasp sting. Remember when we explored under your house in search of crayfish, and we came across that strange big pinecone?"

"But it wasn't a pinecone, was it?" Yercy giggled. "Well, I have an idea. Let's imagine a bowl sitting between us."

"What? Do I have to?"

Yercy laughed. "Now, this bowl is special, because it's filled with warm sweet honey, bright orange honey, like sugary amber, and it smells like the best cinnamon anyone could ever make. With me?"

"I think so."

"Now, imagine us dipping our hands in. The honey spreads between your fingers, soaking through your bandages, slowly across your skin, warmer and softer with every breath. Breathe in. Breathe out. Each new moment is better than the one before, and *with* each moment, the honey absorbs into your skin. As the honey vanishes, its warmth remains, lingering with sweet cinnamon."

Lola saw her counterpart smile as the imagery concluded. Around them, people moved like particles stuck within a bleached-out tableau. Some clustered in groups, talking, while others floated like debris washed up by the tide. She moved to listen in on one such cluster for curiosity's sake, but the static flickering of her body meant her time back in time was up, for now.

And so, after her visit in the hospital, Lola was in the dreamworld again, or Sweven, as she called it now. Sweven's environment had undergone change once more, its thick sea of oil and polluted atmosphere replaced with clean water and cloudless skies, while the cold metal buildings and towers had changed to marble.

Her eyes peered towards the horizon, blankly at first, then curious about something that had been on her mind for a while now.

How far does it go?

Mute tension filled the air as she walked closer towards the ledge where the sky and sea split along the horizon, though it felt like she was going nowhere at all. It seemed that distance meant little in a place like this. The pale buildings were specks now. She'd passed by them and kept going and going, driven by a need for answers. Lola was oblivious to the water's pull tightening around her ankles. She noticed it only as the sand ramped down, strangely, and lowered her knee deep where the current ran stronger, flowing forth as if a maw waited somewhere ahead, swallowing the tide.

But when she verged on turning back, the ground fell away in a sheer drop that yanked her body hard into the rushing water. Sharp dread prickled her skin as she kicked and flailed against the water's drag in search of footing. At last, her feet dug into an outcrop high enough to stand on. She was soaked and shivering with adrenaline. Through widened eyes somewhat red from the brine, she watched the ocean vanish from view, running down in a cascade off to nowhere. The waterfall rimmed Sweven's border like a huge overflowing bathtub. She saw how it curved into the makings of an island of sorts, a rounded platform suspended within a realm hidden from the universe.

"Then the world separating the timelines is like a huge floating island." Yercy maneuvered her glider near Lola's. "I wonder how it all got there to begin with. Can it even be explained?"

Lola propped against her wave glider's mast, staring into the orange late-afternoon glow shining between cloud puffs gathered ahead, getting lost there.

"Are you alright?"

"Just tired," she said. "Hey, young Yercy and her father visited the hospital earlier. I almost forgot what Brimothy looked like until now. It's been so long. He seemed calm despite all that's happened. I don't remember…Was he ever one for being receptive, you know, open minded?

"Depends. Why?"

"Well, I was wondering if he'd believe my situation if my younger self told him about it. So far, no one except us will buy into things like time travel or Sweven, and that goes for both timelines. Surely your father would be different, right?"

"With some luck, perhaps. Father often read me fairy tale scripts before bed. Some were completely nonsensical and I wouldn't understand them until some years later, but his way of expressing things always pulled through when a story went off the deep end. So, there's that. He's usually been pretty agreeable, even through my preteen years. But as for our situation? I'm not placing any bets."

Lola's unsureness led her eyes back towards the oncoming dusk. A coastline unlike any other approached them now, a band marking the skyline with glimmering pinpoints of light, like grains of gemstones. Her map named it Honeydew Cape in bold cursive calligraphy.

"If my navigation isn't fuzzy," Lola said, "there's a path somewhere along this cape that leads further inland—the next leg on our route towards Stalactite Cove."

Night had fallen when their hulls finally scraped the shoreline, and their feet kissed the sand that glowed with a subtle aura of golden luminescence. From here, Fervine's coast would blend into the scenery farther inland before disappearing completely; terrain undisturbed by time. Most had no reason to venture past the islands like this because there were no trade routes, native towns, or anything of the sort, at least not on the coast directly. This knowledge brought an odd, eerie calm around Lola's thoughts as a humid breeze jostled her hair, the smell of the air laden with brine and wet sediment, along with something else—something stale that felt like it was alive, moving without being noticed, breathing without being heard.

Sandcastle Kingdom

*"The elves who live around the Whisper Lakes are said to be the strongest
mages in Strevenfall, having achieved a form of immortality by harnessing
the natural energy present in all living things. It is said they were founded
by one of Kain Nepta's descendants, the merfolk wizard who was present
during the realm's creation."*

- Nerfidalia; a realm historian

As they rationed leftover food into camping bags for the continued
journey overland, Lola gave pause to how Yercy never once objected to
leaving their sailboats behind for the eventual trip back. It was not
guaranteed the gliders would still be there if left unattended.

The shore was too soft to mount shelter on; their efforts inevitably
ended with the tent somersaulting towards the waves. Lola questioned if
tents were even necessary until Yercy noted the sand spiders. A unanimous
decision was made to sleep further upland despite the insects. Though in
truth, their reluctance came more from not hearing the ocean as clearly
rather than the risk of being bitten.

Lola almost smiled. "Can we believe ourselves? Still bothered over
insignificant things, like children."

"We can afford it," said Yercy. "It's not as if someone's watching over our shoulders. Hardly a soul lives here, except us, and we don't even live here. I'd never even heard about Honeydew Cape until you mentioned it."

"It's quite the opposite of Garenham. Few places there offer full privacy at all."

Before long they'd settled near a clump of bamboo shoots wobbling against the midnight breeze. A campfire crackled between them.

"So, what's Garenham like anyway?" Yercy asked between bites of fruit. "Father always described that city's passion for stained glass. The campus itself is basically made of the stuff, right?"

Lola replied, "More or less, but it's also everything else, and everything happens at once."

"Meaning what?"

"For one, Garenham's the most populated city in Strevenfall by far. You couldn't find an empty street, one not crowded with passersby, at least during the day. People are always working through their tight schedules, myself included. Life's been split between the campus and Sandy's Diner ever since I turned twenty, two years ago. Maybe that's what places like Garenham are made for."

Yercy caught the sharpness ending her phrase.

"Which is why nighttime became my favorite solace," Lola went on, "especially during full moons. I would go beyond city borders and perform those songs that stuck with me through the years, or songs I drafted myself, either for a school assignment or just out of curiosity. Remember when we took dance lessons as teenagers? I would've sworn my routine years were over, but the hills there offer plenty of room to move around while playing my violin."

"Sounds beautiful."

She nodded. "But it sounds like a rush despite that. Horse carriages come in droves through the promenades, particularly during first light. I made a good choice in picking out an apartment that was at least tucked some ways off from the commotion. Perhaps it's instinct—finding refuge where commotion can't find me. At least it's productive, right?"

"I wouldn't know." Yercy fed an apple core to the fire. "Seems counterintuitive"

"Counterintuitive?"

"I mean the commotion. Wouldn't that make less sense if people wanted things done? One might think calmer settings would do just that, not the opposite. You know, like patios and boardwalks, or quiet beaches."

"If such places were hosts to music classes, I wouldn't have moved out."

Yercy didn't speak, letting the phrase swim aimlessly between their eyes, with her own eyes peacefully leveled in a way that made the silence deepen.

Lola blinked away.

"So why didn't you write to me all these years?"

"What?"

"I'd never heard anything from you ever since we'd parted years ago, unless the city's rapid pace has absolutely no time to spare on leisure. Which, honestly, could be true from how you're describing things."

Lola searched her thoughts for the right phrase, something natural and cordial, but replied in a hurry. "I...I wasn't prepared for *that* question, honestly."

"Am I asking out of turn?"

"No! It's...like I said, managing time is hard on a busy schedule, and Garenham isn't lenient to people who want it any other way. No one can expect consistency either. Also..." Her train of thought lapsed. "I'm sorry. These sound like petty excuses."

"Maybe, but only you know for sure, not me."

A breeze jostled the fire, embers whirling up in a soft spiraling dance.

"I-I can drop the matter for now," said Yercy. "You already have plenty to think about."

Lola's smile was faint, the favor accepted with an awkward pause. She settled down across her bed roll. "So, what about you?"

"Me?"

"From what I've seen, you essentially have complete freedom around the sailboat shop now. That couldn't have happened overnight."

"Well, that goes in large part to a generous employer, and even then, gaining Brishon's unconditional trust took years of commission work before he allowed materials for my personal projects. We were a small property back then as well, so I was mostly needed to fulfill customer orders until more people jumped on board. Now we're practically living off our own creations, where people come to us and buy what *we* make." Yercy nodded down shore. "Those two smaller vessels were actually in my portfolio last year."

"The two we used in getting here?" asked Lola.

"Yes. I spent about five weeks getting them both from raw components to something usable, not including test runs. Brishon's personal lessons on woodcraft lent me some great advice when it seemed like nothing was going right. And of course, my father was always open to talk, even when he moved into a smaller home once I'd bought my own." Yercy noticed something amiss in the way Lola's glance was averted but continued anyway. "Though, he wasn't too thrilled by my choices at first. After all, getting salaries from a new establishment poses obvious risks. Maybe his worry still lingers today, but at least we know each other enough that debating over the subject is wasted words, and that moving on is what's best."

"Oh, come on."

Yercy leaned back, patiently curious.

"Please, don't get the wrong impression. I believe you, but surely no one who spends five weeks making *two* sailboats would be content with leaving them behind without second thoughts."

"So, you only have doubt, not disbelief."

"Confusion would describe it better. I'm just…confused is all."

Yercy was relaxed despite the sincerity of Lola's tone, as if implying her answer would be carefree, playful even. "I might sound half my age here, but in some ways, woodcraft reminds me of building sandcastles." She paused, smiling. "Suppose my life goes on as planned. It's certain I'll end up making hundreds of different vessels, but most will be sold off and used by others anyways. If owning them was important, I would've become a collector before anything else. Sandcastles are much the same. The real luxury comes from building them because everyone knows they'll disappear once high tide arrives."

"A mindset like that seems vital in your career," said Lola.

"Well, that, and my signature is engraved on pretty much everything I make." Yercy nestled into her own bed roll across from Lola's, hair strands sliding like painted threads down her face. She added softly, "But worrying about it isn't necessary. I'm just glad my sailboats didn't capsize during our time at sea."

Their campfire's sedating warmth ensured that neither of them stayed awake much longer, but Lola roused again just a few hours later after midnight, right on schedule. She was nearly taken by surprise at how the silence felt thickened, like submerging her ears in water, a sensation likely caused by the lack of nocturnal wildlife in this part of the area. It brought a special type of comfort, though. Nothing could stop her thoughts as they swam in lucid arrays, free from reality's constant flow of events, even if temporarily.

Straying from her friend's companionship was especially dangerous at night, but Lola was adamant about killing time after exhausting other chores like bathing and cleaning the navigation equipment. She carried her violin where the terrain flattened into a stage-like area, providing ample playing room. Particles fluttered as she curved through the sand's embrace with gentle whirls and pivots, her footprints marking its surface, moving harmoniously with each note, relaxed, at ease, until a fleeting thought spurred the moment.

So why didn't you write to me all these years?

125

The rhythm drained as she paused and stared absently where her tracks had blemished the stage. A breeze tried nudging her back into motion, to no avail.

So, it's not clear yet? Just look at me. Her lips pressed together. *Why would someone like me, whose life is stuck with panic, reach out to someone like you, whose life couldn't get any better?*

At dawn the next day, as the girls trekked further along the coast, flocks of birds—both familiar and not—passed overhead, including petrels with lime-green feathers and ribbon-like tails.

"We're really getting no shortage of novel creatures around here," said Yercy, but Lola's attention was fixed towards the map. "Hey, our route can't be that puzzling."

"Oh, sorry," Lola said, forcing a grin.

"You seem distracted, or tired."

"I'm fine. I think these birds indicate we're nearing more forested areas. My map puts us around Honeydew Cape's midway point. It should be about a five-day hike from here to the path that cuts inland, to the forests themselves. How are we doing on food?"

Yercy checked their bag. "Five pears. A few apples. Some peaches. More than enough potatoes. And about five handfuls of nuts and berries. Though we're lacking fish—we ran out some days ago."

"No matter. There seems to be a township edged into the forest path roughly eight kilometers in. I believe it's a place called Sillstone." Lola pointed out where the simple depictions of rooftops meant her statement was feeble at best, but she quickly mentioned that forest streams likely had fish anyway, so they would be fine.

"So, we're using common knowledge as our last resort?" Yercy laughed. "We left the casting rods behind for lighter travel, and neither of us know a lick about spearfishing. Or did Garenham offer classes on outdoor survival?"

"It doesn't matter," she replied shortly, and louder than usual. "No other way gets us to Stalactite Cove within two months."

"Oh, alright," Yercy murmured. Her companion's mind seemed elsewhere in thought today, more so than usual, but the way her balance swayed now proved it was a different problem entirely. Then it hit.

"Is it happening again?" Yercy asked but was already bracing to catch Lola as she staggered and fell limply in her arms, nearly falling herself.

Act Restless, Be Careful, Think Softly

"The sulfur lakes scattered across Zesh's northern dunes are among the realm's deepest bodies of water. It might take an iron plate eight hours to reach the bottom."

- Belver; a native of Zesh

Lola paused midway through Sweven's dreamscape, the faint rustle of her pace diminished slowly until she stood without movement, the ripples cast by her feet dissolving into glass. She'd been doing this recently on every trip between timelines, taking a few moments to halt and embrace the stillness offered by its mystical scenery. Here, all was calm.

But where is here?

Sweven's function as a rift separating past and present was clear, yet that failed to explain much else, especially why it looked as such—a floating island doused in water that never ran dry, and with features undergoing constant change. Like now, as she noticed that in addition to the crumbled white buildings, several lily pads were floating leisurely across the surface, some bearing flowers. Lily pads did not grow in saltwater, yet here they were.

She held one high, watching as water funneled down its leaves and along her arms like ribbons. There was something entrancing about this world's behavior. One could simply sit back and admire how senseless everything was, getting lost in the shapes and abstractions sprouting up at random.

"Feels nice," she said, as her mind echoed, *familiar*.

"Hi again!" The girl hopped off the bed. "My morning checkup thingy took forever this time. People were going in and out and looking at my hands and asking question after question, but today someone asked about Tinman Tom. I never thought anyone here would be interested in anything that didn't involve my hands, or medicine. Of course, no one believed my answer. Why can't adults believe in time travel?"

Lola slouched against the wall. "Typically, *no one* believes in time travel, not even children."

"Why not? Yercy's a child and she knows I'm telling the truth. And what about Bedman Berry?"

"Who's Bedman Berry again?"

"My bed, silly."

"Oh, right," she whispered drowsily.

"While they changed my bandages today, I imagined this place as an underwater castle, and Bedman Berry was my magic throne surrounded by treasure piles stacked really high. Meanwhile, Tinman Tom acted as a guard protecting our treasure." The girl went on filling the room with aquatic scenery, coral reefs, mermaids, words spreading like magic, until she slowed into a distracted mutter, before stopping completely.

"Don't have much energy?" asked Lola. "These sleep cycles have worn me out too."

"No, I'm just remembering what happened after my checkup, though I really don't want to. People were whispering outside my castle, not only nurses, but someone I know, and the voice frightened me. She sounded very polite and looked very fancy, but she must be angry about what happened—angry that I can't practice anymore."

Lola was on the verge of asking who but stopped as the realization hit; an explosion of peafowl makeup splattered on a face deceptively gentle. "Mother," she frowned, heading for the door.

"Where are you going?"

"Don't move." She crept into the hallway where lights beamed their pallid glares. The passing attendants strained her footwork as she maneuvered past them and towards the lobby one floor below, a place teeming with bodies caught within a colorless atmosphere. Her eyes skimmed for Evelyn's hue-swollen dress. Nothing stood out, particles wading among blanched white, until a painted smear was spotted just as it left out the entry doors.

Don't ever return. Her thoughts screamed on replay. *Ever, ever!*

"Was it her?" the girl asked when Lola returned to the room, pulling her blankets up.

Lola didn't answer. She didn't have to.

"Why did Ma come here?"

"Not sure. Why would she even bother? You can't play the violin now, and it's surely not for sentimental reasons."

They allowed the calm in the space between them to expand, stretching each moment until their nervousness thinned away. Footsteps from outside mumbled through the drywall like vibrations submerged in stream water.

Lola rose mutely, motioning her counterpart to follow as she said, "Come on. Being caged indoors must get stale for you. Let's go out."

There was a garden strewn about the hospital's yard outside, bright clean walkways weaving through bushes with flower vines twining overhead, sunlight filtering down in bands, luring the two raven-haired drifters as they neared its embrace. A runnel glimmered below the overpass leading in, breaking into smaller rivulets among the green. They went along, trying to ignore every couple or crowd who passed near, several pausing at the sight of the little girl walking alone with mittens for hands and no one to watch over her, the girl who smiled sheepishly at those concerned enough to ask about her hands—or anything else.

"What happened?"

"Are you lost?"

"Need help?"

Such questions were left unanswered.

"Just find someplace quiet," said Lola, "where others can't bother us."

One path led into an arboretum detached from the main avenue, a nursery for flowers and ferns held together by vines branching off stone fixtures. A fountain sparkled near the center. Lola sat against it while her counterpart launched on a mission to smell every flower in sight. Birds sang. Petals danced. She wondered if serene moments like these lasted longer for children.

The girl stopped. "Hey, isn't this what parents do?"

Lola blinked in confusion.

"I always see kids and adults walking together around here, and I always thought about where they could be heading off to. Is this where they go?"

"When it's warm like today, maybe," she said. "Or maybe they go somewhere to eat, or somewhere beyond city borders where the valleys are. It's common that families do what we're doing, and when you're older, you could even go by yourself. I would spend days on end traveling around Fervine before leaving. Sure enough, nice places like these attract all kinds of people."

"Traveling? To where?"

"Anyplace with a good sense of paradise. Places without much noise. On some mornings I'd visit Fervine's parks and practice new songs before the town had even woken up. Sometimes, my searches for new playing locations brought me to some of the most obscure parts of town— abandoned castles, old cabins, even meadows that innkeepers swore were haunted, though I never witnessed anything off. Strevenfall's track record for the paranormal is less than other realms."

"Did you perform for other people?"

"No, just me mostly," Lola said. Valery always used that term, perform, as a mantra, a weapon.

The girl nestled beside her. Their postures mirrored, legs folded in, arms clasped around them. "Hey, what happens to me? As in me growing up."

"I can't say," she replied. "We've changed so much about your timeline."

"Well, what happened to *you*?"

She pursed her lips, thinking. "To put it one way, my aptness for the violin never stopped. Even as I learned more instruments in later years—piano, flute, trumpet—the violin always drew me back into playing it. Even Yercy grew concerned about me spending hours and hours studying music catalogs and other texts, some whose word count surpassed most dictionaries—and not the small kind. Before long, I'd received letters from universities upland. I was among the few whom Garenham requested personally onto their campus, and fewer still who completed the entrance exam without flaws." She looked skyward, fountain drops dotting her face. "In short, life became music, always practicing to better my sound, my posture, my technique—everything."

The girl noticed Lola's mouth pressed into a line, matched with what looked like droplets clinging to her. Water from the fountain?

"I...never stopped."

"Oh," the girl whispered. "So, when I get better, will my life be music too? What about Ma? She always wants my music. People always want it, and it hurts."

"Don't worry," said Lola. "I'll be there."

"What?"

She cupped her mouth as if something dire had escaped, but doing so was painful, too painful. "Don't worry," she echoed, because nothing else felt right. "I'll be there. No one has the right to take advantage of you. So,

I'll stay as long as you want, and protect *your* rights from others who'd try to take them."

"Are you sure? As long as I want?"

"Quite sure, now let's head back. My time here is nearly over."

A few passersby caught sight of the girl heading out as she walked hand in hand beside a dew-covered silhouette; a vaporiform figure guiding her steps.

Is that a ghost? one thought.

Is she being haunted? thought another.

All of them gave the girl space, perhaps fearing the apparition beside her.

The inland path was a vein edged into the trees and thickets beyond, a faint trail that likely hadn't seen travelers in ages. Lola would have passed right by it if not for her map coordinates. Cypress vines partly concealed the entrance like a mouth choked on nature, thorn bushes lining either side.

"Not a charming path by any means," Lola sighed wearily.

Yercy rummaged through their bags. "Thankfully, we brought tougher clothes for these situations. Right now, anything beats tank tops and bathing suits, and our hair might need tying up. I can already hear the insects in droves."

And sure enough, the path was frenzied with life chorusing among trees whose branches canopied the sky. Their steps fumbled over splayed roots and weeds, the trail overgrown by the years and a lack of visitors. A twisted ankle was just about guaranteed if one trekked carelessly. But the trunks—the huge trunks of trees fallen across the trail led to many misadventures of climbing over or somehow traveling around, getting lost at times, other times landing ungracefully off another redwood log. Moving along the more easily traversable spans of forest, however, Lola caught her friend's poise on even ground, how the nereid walked with each step spilling into the next as if carried by a fluid energy.

Look at me, she thought. *I'm nothing like you.*

The vegetation soaked in the nighttime's chilled dampness, which made sleeping a challenge. Lola never ventured out during these hours despite yearning to. Instead, she would curl up and listen as wildlife chattered outside the tent. Occasionally, her focus went elsewhere, sometimes towards Yercy, even if she was aware that observing people while they slept was improper at the least, and invasive at most. Their bed rolls had been placed close together in efforts to share body heat. Yercy's frame moved at every breath drawn through parted lips, perhaps dreaming about magic light builds or bottled ships coasting on air. She watched, wondering if she'd ever sleep like that again, enough to get lost in dreams.

As the days passed, Lola's mind was adrift, remembering the girl's conversation about life and music, about those who'd steal both if given the chance—about her promise. Her eyes, meanwhile, seemed to wander aimlessly across the scenery. Oceanic brooks sparkled among the forested panorama surrounding them. Water lilies paraded past: a floral flotilla.

A fresh, dewy breeze touched Lola as they navigated the trail's next bend, bringing her more to attention. The river running beside them spilled into a crater-shaped lagoon further ahead, the water clean, possibly filtered by rocks, its surface glazed with late-morning sunshine.

"It'd be a crime not to enjoy ourselves here," Yercy said, "even if we're sick of bathing suits."

Lola watched her companion dive off overhangs and surface minutes later while she waded near the calmer side where the depths reached only shoulder height. She remained faraway in mind, however, regardless of the lush scenery and soothing water.

An approaching weather front stopped the pastime early. Rain pattered the trees as they left, puddles reflecting their soured expressions towards waterlogged clothes, even if Yercy cared less than others would. She walked on steadily until the footsteps behind her lagged, then vanished, because her companion had stopped.

"Anything wrong?"

"Why did this happen to me?" Lola said. "The time traveling, 'Hummingbird's Verse', all that?"

"I can't say. There are forces beyond our control." Yercy couldn't meet her eyes, so she looked off instead. "I suppose you've thought about it…a lot."

"At least more so than before. My younger self asked about her future recently, as if I could answer aside from explaining my own. Most people expect that she'll die before the summer, or at least lose her hands, and when that doesn't happen, what? Would my parents resume doll training? If anything, they'll be obsessing over her even more, and if not, well…" She rolled her eyes. "*Valery* surely will."

"You sound like it'll never end."

Lola didn't react.

"Yet we know matters lighten up eventually. After all, you're here, right?"

"But does that mean enough? I've changed the other timeline's future so much that it may end up differently."

They started walking again before Lola continued.

"And who's to say these forces can't be controlled when I've controlled them plenty? Surely, more can be done besides chaperoning the girl until we find her antidote."

Yercy paused briefly. "Implying what?"

"Her future will likely return to what it was before unless I intervene, because once the Pern family realizes their daughter's been cured, they'll be making plans to abuse her talent, never mind abusing *her*. My actions could do wonders in revising the timeline given enough perseverance. If there's—"

Yercy turned suddenly. "Why!"

Lola jerked, having never known her to shout so abrasively.

"Forgive me." She covered her mouth. "I was under the impression that we'd treat your—her—condition after leaving Stalactite Cove."

"Is it worth just treating, though?"

135

"...Lola."

"My other self deserves more than being cured of the illness I helped cause."

"Lola!"

"What?"

"Don't you care more about treatment, rather than changing her past into something else? So why pursue the latter after the former's already been straightened out?"

"Because just leaving behind my younger self after she's cured is careless and wasteful. 'Hummingbird's Verse' didn't bridge our timelines for nothing." Their eyes met finally. "Why are you against this?"

Yercy replied, "Even if you're right, that doesn't make what you're *planning* right."

For several moments, there were only the sounds of rain tapping on leaves.

"Mother came by," said Lola, "meaning she hasn't been found to be a woman who abuses her child, and once the virus dies, one can only imagine the self-satisfied smirk she'll have locking my younger self in the house. The future seems pretty certain from there, or is a reminder in order? Evelyn had me play naked, had me play until blood was drawn from my fingers, had Father stick me with electricity, had Valery watch me whenever they thought something—*anything*—undermined their expectations. They all humiliated, tortured, deceived, and did so eagerly. So, let's not debate over the ethics, right or wrong." She walked ahead, almost brushing Yercy's arm. "We'll mount shelter until the rain stops. A tarp blanket over some branches will do."

Five hours slipped by before the sunlight returned, during which the nereid found no conversation. Her feet felt heavy as they changed clothes between a tarpaulin drape. "We need to talk about this," she muttered, and couldn't choose between relief or fret when Lola stayed quiet, seemingly not hearing.

The forest life took on more predatory forms further ahead. Lavender tree bulbs released their poisonous spores, scattering like upturned feathers. Strange animalistic plants moved autonomously in search of insects, jaws glistening with nectar. Roots latticed the uneven trail marred by dents and pockets. Lola staggered and fell when her foot caught beneath one. She nearly fell again as Yercy helped her to stand.

"Probably sprained. Just my luck."

Yercy looked it over. "You should rest. We haven't done so for hours anyway."

"No. Our passage here won't take much longer, only about half an hour left. The town of Sillstone can't be far now."

Yercy leaned her against a tree. "Don't be ridiculous. The ground's slippery from the rain." They sat, and the break in motion would have given room for repartee if Yercy wasn't so concerned. "We need to talk about this."

"My ankle?" Lola asked with a feigned, quizzical look, but dropped the act. "I heard you the first time around. My choice remains. I've already promised to carry it out."

"What could change your mind?"

"A miracle—if those exist—but I'm not expecting one."

Yercy tried abating the tension with her words, then a kind look, struggling at both. "You know, I've realized something lately."

Lola turned to look at her.

"In times like these, my head keeps asking itself, 'What should I say?' or 'What am I supposed to say?' Seems proper, right? Yet what's funny is that it's useless anyhow because the answer's already been with me. And guess what's also funny? Even if I know what to say, I can't say it, or rather, I ought not to."

"Why not?"

"Oh...never mind. At least imagery can cheer things up. Remember our light bulb? Let's envision it again, how the liquid builds and recedes, and changes color."

She went along despite being flustered over the nereid expressing her curiosity only to drop the subject soon after, and pressing the matter wouldn't help. One bulb formed, filling up, another glowing from within, folding out as a flicker snapped between them, followed by lightheaded fatigue, the past uttering its call.

Yercy didn't move when Lola slouched against her, unconscious. She watched the rain puddles curl as birds drank from them. "Here you go again," she said, "launching back in time where the pain is, always getting involved with things long gone." She looked down, her sun hat obscuring her eyes. "Not much room left for my take, is there? What happened back then didn't just affect you...but sharing that might worsen your troubles even more."

Pale light poured through the room's entry—blanching the girl's face—as it stretched over the mattress where she lay. And when a figure crossed the doorway, her fearful eyes widened as they took in the sight of skin wrapped in peafowl clothes.

Lola gripped the bedpost, eyes narrowed.

Evelyn sat in the furthest chair; her hands knitted together in a tight bridge below her chin. Her legs were not crossed, instead planted firm as if to withstand a sudden force. Her gaze was tilted down for a time before she looked back up. "Lola."

"Yes ma'am?" the girl said.

After a lingering pause, Evelyn spoke. "I've lost count of the days you've been here. How strange life can be without my daughter around." The peafowl hadn't breathed yet. "So strange in fact, that I couldn't resist visiting."

"You needn't say a word." Lola's grip tightened on the bedpost. "Mother deserves no answer."

The girl nodded, letting the silence draw.

"My husband warned that coming here might only hurt the situation. He's always so timid. What kind of parent leaves their child alone with

138

strangers? Very improper. Children always need fostering." Evelyn went on chirping about maternal love—how much better it was compared to any other—and about Valery suddenly leaving town for professional reasons, oftentimes repeating what she said or reiterating them differently. A disembodied movement snapped her out of her monologue, one of the bedposts shuddering. "Child, aren't you listening?"

The silence lengthened.

"Let me see those hands." Evelyn went to the girl's bedside but had yet to touch them. A ghostly presence stopped her; floor creaks and disembodied marks pressed into the mattress, then a weight in the air drained the room of its little sounds.

"I don't wanna go home," the girl whispered.

The room suddenly clamored with flung papers and chairs ramming towards the woman whose face filled in terror. Lola was shouting, but only the girl could hear her voice as her older self raked objects from shelves and countertops, her nails bleeding and breaking from the force of her grip, her anger, her hate.

Evelyn had fled.

Lola was panting.

The girl quivered, watching her counterpart stand over the mess, a shadowy form in contrast.

Synthesize

"… Branches push us apart where weakness shows. So, let's pin back our ears and listen to the ways we keep things unsaid, the forest changed. We never used to glimpse beyond the trees. Now I've felt leaves soak up my fears as we whisper down the hills where the lampposts hum. Dawn swept a night's cloak aside to see where nature's kept us secret, singing of city roads few can ever tame. The people are many. The buildings are loud. Listlessly, the owls fall back as birds take their place. You've gambled to see us here with every taken chance. Brambles in your stomach tell that our fears may show even as the seasons change…"

- "Hummingbird's Verse"; lyrics part 2

Water filled between Lola's toes as she crawled through blackness, the kind that crippled more than sight alone, the kind that magnified the shock of vertigo with its sheer weightless mass. She felt around, finding her legs, and stood shakily, catching a metallic scent heavy on the air. Droplets of something unknown ran down her thighs.

I'm naked.

Her eyes adjusted, or perhaps the void was dissipating on its own. Apprehension replaced shock when figures loomed overhead, then around, ascribing the scene with odd, strangely familiar outlines. Nausea replaced vertigo when the ripples caused by her movements reflected red—crimson red—and felt nearly glutinous once she lifted a palm's worth for inspection.

Lightheaded, she almost couldn't feel the blood slipping away, smearing her arms, and she took several steps back as if met by a dangerous animal. Sharp fear crept in like thorns pinching her nerves, painful yet numbing. The figures appeared taller, or really, they appeared more like smaller ones clumped into large piles, piles of yarn, cloth, and plastic. Voices bristled in the air, biting her ears with mechanical hum and chatter starting low, then louder, throwing horrible names that wouldn't let up or jeers aimed where her dignity was weakest. Her breathing became more rapid. Each take of air pressed against those before, and her throat clenched now, her teeth gritting. Speaking out was vanity. Vanity deserved punishment.

Daylight brushed across Lola's face as she awoke to an unfamiliar ceiling, the kind that softened the haze nightmares often left behind, though not completely. She sat up and steadied the hammering in her chest. A nearby window beamed morning into the white cedar room.

I'm in a bed, in a cabin.

The window looked out across a valley sculpted by rolling hills, decorated with flower beds and willow trees whose branches hung like curtains. Mill ponds sparkled among them, reflecting clouds and blue skies. The view would have been incredible if her memory wasn't tracing back. Recalling the bad dream was fretful, but then her memory traced farther—papers scattering as Evelyn scampered away.

"It couldn't have happened differently." A faint murmur.

Lola was hobbling towards the door when it opened suddenly enough to scare her. A rusty-haired elven boy popped in and raced out, yelling, "Mom, she's awake!" A stirring of commotion came from downstairs, followed by a minty-haired elven woman approaching the doorway, who reached out before the Lola could stagger or trip.

"Not so fast, miss. Better stay off that foot until a doctor sees it. And please tie up your gown. We have kids here."

"Where am I?" asked Lola.

"Sillstone Valley. We've been tending you since yestereve."

"Thank you."

The woman laughed incredulously. "Oh, don't thank me. Your friend carried you for what had to be hours before making it out of the forest. Never thought I'd see a nereid and a human paired together, both whose rarity speak for themselves."

Lola was served bread cakes and strawberries while sunshine warmed her bed sheets. The young woman's name was Pearl, mother of twins and with a spouse currently out pruning the town's wisteria gardens. It felt unnatural having a mother treat her like this, especially at daybreak when she was once expected to bathe, dress, clean, and set up for practice before the next hour had arrived—all while expecting punishment everywhere between—never mind breakfast.

Pearl noticed her staring at a parrot doll nearby. "Anything wrong?"

"No, not at all. Is Yercy here?"

"My husband showed her to the market strip on his way out. She talked regarding low food rations and something for the valley sun. Very generous, that one."

Sillstone's healer arrived with two supply kits and careful hands tracing Lola's foot in search of fractures. The injury ended up being several pulled ligaments, one of which had almost torn upon falling. Days of traveling across uneven ground, in sandals no less, had certainly played its role. Several gauze rounds and a shoe-sized brace would ensure a week-long recovery, the shortest estimation possible.

"You were watching her intensely," Pearl said afterwards. "Glaring even."

"My experience with doctors hasn't been pleasant lately."

Outside, the morning breeze fluttered Lola's marigold sundress. It was among the last of the clean apparel left in her bag as just about everything

142

else had been stained with forest mud. She'd chosen a short walking staff over a crutch despite the suggestion that she shouldn't be walking at all. A fruit wagon lent easy transport along Sillstone's roads placed upon the hills. She joined several others riding into the town square.

"So, what can you tell me about this place?" she asked no one specifically.

"We're the break separating Honeydew Cape's coastal woods and the prairie beyond," a young man informed her. "Most come here to rest after traveling a good way, kinda like what you're doing, I suppose. Nearly all the lovely maidens here are elven." He looked down the road. "New faces are easily spotted."

Her eyes followed the man's line of sight. Yercy sauntered down the trail ahead. Once Lola got off to meet her and the wagon left, they were alone on the now quiet road, surrounded by a beautiful vista.

"You...carried me out of the forest."

"We arrived at dusk. Thankfully, Mr. Kernot—that's Pearl's husband—discovered us soon after crossing town borders." Yercy laughed sheepishly. "I'd nearly fainted by then. Our bags might've weighed more than you."

Lola noticed her arms. "Speaking of bags."

"It's mostly food, but I also found these." Yercy unwrapped the parasols and folded one out, light glowing through translucent teals and blues patterned gracefully. "The prairie isn't kind to those without personal shade, and sun hats can only do so much. This one's yours."

Lola held it, almost feeling the colors paint her skin. "Would thanking you even suffice now? It must've been torturous bringing me and the supplies here. And the parasol is beautiful."

"Well, I actually made two trips."

"Thank you for everything."

Yercy smiled and unfolded her own parasol of lime dancing with chartreuse. It was a different smile, guarded perhaps.

143

Night fell, and when Lola played her violin this time around, "Hummingbird's Verse" sounded off-key from weeks of neglected tuning, such that its magic failed. A lantern provided the light dusk had taken from Pearl's spare bedroom. Tightening strings D and G brought cleaner notes, restoring the song's magic once more. The girl appeared nearby.

Lola reached out.

The girl looked away.

Lola retracted slowly. "Were you frightened back then?"

"Maybe, just a little."

"Was...I the one frightening you?"

"Just a little, maybe." Their eyes met. "Do fingernail beds heal? I asked and a doctor said yes, but it takes forever."

Lola regarded her fingers and paused, each one capped by nails that were chipped or clotted, if not both.

The girl, bashfully, moved close to see the blood pockets underneath. "At least your other hand's still pretty."

"I can't believe no one noticed all day, me included." Lola turned, still finding distance between them. "Please don't be afraid. If your mother—our mother—returns, I'll try not to worsen things more, okay?"

Her counterpart smiled and sat closer. It was a different smile, cautious perhaps.

Another day had arrived. The town mingled with bright tapestry and fruit stands lined across the storefronts, two streaks of color bridged by a road wide enough for eight side-by-side wagons. Lola was relieved to find far fewer crowds than Garenham. Light filtered down in shades of bright yellow and beige as they passed beneath the rain drapes.

Yercy pointed. "And here's where they mend gardening tools. The physician's building shouldn't be far."

Lola was first to step inside, and the appointment began before long. She hardly moved as the practitioner twisted a syringe through her nails, reliquifying the blood for extraction.

"I've never seen anyone try that without anesthetics," one nurse said.

"High tolerance, from my childhood."

Their visit concluded as the pressure beneath Lola's nails alleviated. Next, they leased a wagon and ventured towards Sillstone's outer hills, rolls of ryegrass on which tributaries flowed. The landscape flattened further ahead, an emerald plain spreading wider than eyes could see as the town's border blurred into lands farther still. The flora was alive with aspen trees of Strevenfall's brightest yellow. Several formed a tunnel leading somewhere, someplace unknown, just the road and aspens creating a mysterious entry.

"One might say we're lost," said Lola. "Namely me."

Yercy grinned. "My sightseeing trip this morning provided wonders. Wait and see."

She needn't wait long, however. The path of trees opened, and the proceeding landscape was at first overwhelming until her eyes adjusted to the brighter sunlight. Rows upon rows of wisteria trees cascaded across a verdant field as if knowing no bounds, branches thriving with hues spilling down like strokes of paint suspended overground. The array of colors stretched from cool white at one far end of the field to the warmer tones of pink at the other. They arrived in the middle, on yellow and lime green harmonized by every possible shade of the flora married together.

Lola carefully climbed out, looking around, mostly up. "Pearl mentioned these gardens. Sillstone's very own wisteria."

"I heard it's better when explored barefoot," said Yercy. "The grass is Velvet Rye, our realm's softest."

Fleece-tailed parrots eyed them curiously from atop a branch, speaking broken language to the horticulturists who were busy cutting sprigs.

"Pretty ladies! Pretty ladies!" one parrot chirped.

"Love taps, lovely be!" chirped another.

There was a spot between lilac purple and violet offering less noise. Lola sat against a tree while Yercy sprawled over the grass near it. Either could have slept outside comfortably, but not amid such lavish groves worth staying awake in.

The nereid turned, head propped on her elbow. "How's *my* child self doing?"

"She's visited several times thus far," said Lola. "She's normally cheerful, although worried like everyone else, or at least those who care."

A long pause, then, "Have you ever seen my child self after those visits?"

"Well, no."

"What about after our play dates on the beach, when we were kids?"

"It might be invasive to watch an unsuspecting girl," she said. "Why'd you ask?"

Yercy settled back to bird gazing, one leg folded over the other's knee. "I was just wondering, privacy notwithstanding."

Departing from the garden instilled fond veneration, akin to rising from a daydream. One horticulturist waved them over as he descended off a branch pulley. He was a slim man with sable hair that had a little curl to it, and, surprisingly, he was human.

"Miss Pern, yes? I've already met Miss Rivitine." He smiled modestly. "Certainly, my wife's breakfast did the stomach justice. She never mentioned your added hand injury."

Lola glanced at her bandages.

"They came overnight," Yercy cut in. "They're not worth fretting over, Mr. Kernot."

At the house, Pearl's twins, Lance and Copper, played games under a willow tree's curtains near the house. They moved like two flaxen swathes carried by the wind. Both basked in afternoon's embrace, time a countless measure. Lola watched them earnestly, yet not quite in a motherly way. She was solemn and curious, wistful even.

That night, she was dreaming again, darkness spanned over crimson and words cast like stones against bare skin. Her curiosity drew her several yards closer towards a pile, confirming the dolls lying in mangled heaps.

Holding one made her feel sick. Fear sprouted in her mind when she moved further on, that fear changing into paranoia growing like weeds, getting violent, and it was getting harder to breathe. She awoke sweating, gasping, and leaned off the covers, staff ready, violin in hand, the outdoors in mind.

Although dancing was perilous, Lola could still roost on a hillside facing the night's lunar circle. She eased into a warm lullaby before scaling more intricate compositions. The half-moon's light grazed the wires as they shivered and sounded.

"Is this how you escape?"

Her hair flung as she turned, meeting Yercy's level gaze. Neither moved, nor blinked.

"Odd choice of words." Lola turned back. "Escape from who, exactly?"

"Or what." The nereid sat close to her, really close. "No, sorry for being confrontational, only I've known about your outings since we left Honeydew Cape. It mirrors our teen years when you'd take music trips around town."

"Not just then or now, but everywhere in between."

"So, is it…escapism?"

"Call it peace-finding, preferably under the moon. Crescent. Full. Doesn't matter. This moon kept me company as a child during wakeful nights, and now I find myself doing likewise whenever I feel like it."

"Does it make you feel better?"

"It keeps me from feeling worse."

Yercy grew quiet.

"It's kinda sad, right?" Lola sighed. "Just running off to places like this."

"Of course not! There are plenty of reasons to withdraw sometimes. Who am I to criticize you for this?"

Lola verged on replying, but Yercy had left when she looked over to the now-empty spot beside her.

Copper ran up as Lola cleaned the recently bought food.

"That violin upstairs looks neat. Can we play a song?"

"Please, our guest is busy," said Pearl.

Kernot added, "And keep out of other people's rooms unless granted permission, especially a lady's."

Copper nevertheless beamed at Lola's consent, sitting with her on the porch swing outside. His beige, buttoned shirt wrinkled as they swayed gently, overlooking the yard. The boy held a clarinet, silver key plates wrapped around a burgundy rod.

"An E-flat clarinet, made from rosewood," Lola remarked.

"Whoa, exactly. I only know a few this and thats, and several ditties."

She flipped through his music binder. "How about 'Swinger Fox?'"

They began. Two braids of sonance intertwined, one loosely skimming across reed-produced notes while the other swirled around its bow-stringed partner. Wind carried leaves, swayed curtains, while several amblers looked twice passing by.

"Where'd you learn to play so well?" he asked.

"M-my personal instructor, before I went to university, anyway."

"I bet you practice a lot too."

She nodded vacantly.

"Ma's the one who got me hooked on music. She used to play really big years back when she was with the...Preh—...Puella?"

"Pueyelliv Orchestra."

"Yeah that...Hey, you look deep in thought."

"Sorry." Her feet crossed. "How...how does your mother teach?"

"We practiced every five rotations, or when there's too much rain for outside stuff. She'll show me a scale or a song, nothing fancy so far."

"Doesn't seem frightening. In fact, that seems truly wonderful."

"Why would I be frightened—" Copper gasped. Lola had suddenly fainted and now slumped against him. Yercy arrived quickly at the boy's call and took his place, handing him Lola's instrument before it could drop from her somnolent hands.

Pearl stepped out. "Should we take your partner upstairs?"

"Here's fine. She looks comfortable." Left alone, Yercy noticed their hair interweaving, pastel shades mixed with raven. Although unappreciated by most, when sunlight kissed Lola's strands right enough, they reflected, flawlessly, a deep ultramarine blue. The nereid leaned into Lola's shoulder, moving gradually, rocking the swing, and she whispered near her ear...

Lola was slightly taken aback as she roused to find Yercy napping there, then leaned forward, head in hands.

"Must have nodded off myself," Yercy said, fighting a yawn. "Hopefully you're a *little* less tired now."

"I-I need to be alone."

"Sure...alright." Yercy obliged reluctantly and stopped before leaving. "How did it go?" But her question received no answer.

Rainfall swept the days after, morning cloudbursts followed by mist veiled over Sillstone's scenery. Most were house-ridden until noon. Grass fields glistened, diamonds spraying as Lance chased swallowtails. Copper shrugged at Lola's disinterest to form their duet again as she was intentionally preoccupied with chores, opting for many despite not having to.

Kernot eyed a window that had recently been wiped clean. "We appreciate her helping around the house lately, but did something happen?"

"So much has happened," said Yercy, "far too much."

Every now and then, commotion stirred around the spare bedroom during nightfall.

One night, however, would prove different. Yercy had always slept downstairs since arriving at Sillstone. The loveseat gave more than enough room. She was reading when the stairs made noise. Lamplight touched over Lola's dress, her feet wrapped in sandals, walking staff placed underarm.

"You're going out without the violin?"

Lola nodded. "I was about to, then I wondered if we could walk together, talk."

"Are my shorts and tank top adequate? I'm not planning to get dressed like you."

The open fields wavered as wind brushed their greenery. Lola paced half a step behind the nereid who appeared strangely distracted.

"It must feel great not wearing that foot brace anymore." Yercy didn't look back. "Remarkably, the departure date we planned hasn't changed. Only four days left."

"Indeed," said Lola.

"And thankfully, this town allows carriage leasing outside its borders, only requiring that they be returned within the deadline. A carriage will get us across the steppes in two weeks flat. I've never been to Strevenfall's prairie. Perhaps it's charming even if it lacks trees." She slowed suddenly, almost staggering. "So, why'd you bring us out here as opposed to playing music, alone."

"Talking doesn't need a good reason, does it?" Lola replied carefully.

"I've mostly been prating while you listen."

"Listening is nice."

"Come on. There must be a reason. You've gotten strange since fainting last time. It's worrying, at least for me anyway."

"Typically, I *would* play alone in hopes of alleviating my thoughts," she said, careful again. "However, now I chose this in place of it. So please keep talking. Your voice is peaceful."

Yercy stopped and they were shrouded by a willow tree.

"What?"

"This is no different. Only the means have changed, music swapped with my voice."

"Weren't you bothered by that music?"

Yercy's eyes narrowed.

"Because you've been strange too since interrupting my...peace finding, a few nights ago. Off-like smiles, distant words, not distant...I

150

don't know. Everything's a bit..." Lola made an unreadable gesture. "Let's not argue."

"What thoughts are my voice alleviating?"

"Please, don't ask loaded questions. You know I'm not all together."

"If I'm being taken advantage of, enlighten me again."

"Taken advantage of!"

Yercy swallowed. "Taken advantage."

"Oh, because it's my fault, right? Only I can be held responsible when you know *exactly* how this trip might affect me. You were probably fine with things before leaving the coast. What about tonight, huh? Or yesterday, even? I'd be a damn moron to think nothing's changed. So, spit it out!"

"Please stop being angry."

"Answer!"

The nereid flinched.

"You think I've gotten bitter."

"Stop," Yercy said.

"Bitter and sad." Lola wobbled forwards. "Then, what!"

"Stop!"

"What!"

"Yes, you're bitter!" Yercy shoved her, regretting it instantly. Lola tripped as her foot writhed in pain, cursing. The nereid rushed to offer help.

Lola threw her staff hard against the willow's trunk, the sound sudden and loud, her breaths stifled and fitful.

"I never meant—!"

"You're right, I'm bitter." Lola turned calmly. "With every reason to be."

Yercy felt awkward standing there and sat, feeling doltish instead.

"I'm just bitter, alright?"

They both laid themselves on the grass, neither knowing what to do and hoping that the next moment would calm things down.

Lola noticed a trail had found its way down the nereid's face. "This isn't our first time yelling at each other."

"I know. The last time was years ago. Suppose I forgot what happens when we talk about this long enough."

"No, the only one to blame is me."

"Quit placing everything on yourself!" Yercy paused, sighing. "Excellent, yelled again...I can't see you getting better, because our journey's made it worse, and worse, and worse."

Lola didn't react, wishing she'd never heard such a peaceful, delicate voice strain while its owner strained even more.

They joined Pearl's family at the greenhouse in town, wide embellished halls linked by sunrooms of colossal size. Flowers and fruit hung like ornaments off vines woven neatly overhead. Entire plum trees were found keeping the cabbage plants company. Kernot noticed their guests walk apart, engaging less.

"Has anything gone amiss?" he asked.

"Amiss wouldn't quite describe it," said Lola. "I'm not sure anymore."

Everyone came out bathed in sweat regardless of having worn the correct attire. By now, the twins were shirtless and still rejoiced upon leaving.

"Should've brought my swim top," Yercy remarked, fanning air down her shirt.

Birds sung.

Trees danced.

Rainfall shimmered.

This time, Lola fainted while exchanging the gauze wraps on her hands for new ones and was carried to bed. She came back down at evenfall, eyeing Yercy who ate dinner alone beneath the overhead lamp. Pearl was watching the sunset outside. Kernot and his sons had gone to bed a few minutes ago.

"I watched the younger you after she visited the hospital." Lola's words diminished as she wiped an eye.

Yercy joined her on the stairs, sitting. The calm atmosphere between them made the silence hereon seem necessary. A light bulb formed, folding magic and water and glass collapsing repeatedly.

Lola began to cry. "How long have you felt this way about me?"

"Long, forever in my book."

"Brimothy knew?"

"Father only knew what he saw, not what I felt."

The silence resumed. Breathe. Cumulate. Absolve.

Pearl trimmed Yercy's hair before it could reach her tailbone. Chromatic threads fell.

"We have spare payment," the nereid said.

"Please, keep it for the rest of your journey. I rarely have the pleasure of hosting such helpful guests, and ladies deserve quality grooming after some hard work."

Kernot sipped his mug, smirking. "She's good at cutting hair now, but you should've seen her so-called skills several years ago."

"Pipe it dear." She winked at her husband. "Are you girls still leaving within the next few days?"

"In four days at the most," said Lola. "Although we could actually use more money, which leads to my question."

"Indeed," Kerot mused after listening to her query. "Extra hands are welcomed."

Tending the wisteria gardens paid handsomely. Lola and Yercy worked as horticulturists through each waking hour that day and the next. Afternoons ended with money set to put towards a carriage lease for precisely their estimated time frame to cross Valtinespring, Strevenfall's prairie. Some routine workers questioned Lola's habit of sleeping under broad daylight and were curious when told it was a temporary dream disorder. Even more curious was how this lady acted as if someone else was around on assumedly empty grass. Only Lola knew her younger self was awed by the groves, the girl having never seen such marvelous trees.

They smelled rancid, returning home covered in twigs and petals clinging with dirty sweat. Pearl demanded the two bathe outside instead of showering. Wooden tubs. Water. Soap. Lola wondered if fewer people had privacy concerns before water lines came about.

Her journal had just ten usable pages left at most, moisture having ruined the last twelve. She wrote while leaning against a bedpost, recording nightmares and beautiful moments.

Tonight's last line was, *I've been blind to what Yercy saw in me then, and what she sees in me now. How could I have not known?*

Her dreams that night delivered the same harrowing world of nakedness and dread. She explored trepidatiously, pacing farther than before, fighting the urge to escape when she woke up, finding herself on the verge of stepping outside, hand squeezed around the doorknob. The nereid took them walking to combat Lola's need to escape. Neither argued or even spoke at all.

When the next morning arrived, the staff was discarded, and Copper and Lola played their final duet.

He glowered as their last melody concluded. "I wish y'all weren't leaving. We could've played more songs."

"We'll meet again," Lola said. "You already have a great teacher, much better than what I had."

He smiled. "Really?"

She placed a hand on his shoulder. "Really, and farewell, my friend."

Few sojourned through the carriage mart at sunrise, which meant ample choice of wheels and storage space. They settled on a single horse-drawn wagon; lightweight, comfortable, fit to tolerate long distances if its passengers carried little. Strevenfall had many laws for animals and utility. The horse in question was harnessed without a mouth bit or martingale, commanded by one's voice alone, and it was also required to roam freely between hauls. Feather-maned colts already loved prairie grass, so there wasn't need to buy extra food.

Sillstone shrank into a small speck swallowed down by distance. Dawn aged into a powder-gold aura from the horizon, painting the clouds. The light ran through Lola's parasol, faintly touching her face.

Lola was staring.

"Is my nose gone?" asked Yercy, smirking.

"I heard you on the porch swing."

A lengthened pause. Her pastel eyes veered away. "As in what, exactly?"

"As in heard clearly, every word."

"Oh...oh."

"Would you've said it if I was awake?"

"Are you...dismissing what I said?"

Lola couldn't answer in a way that seemed correct, so she answered honestly instead. "We'll keep it in the air, alright? There's still quite some time ahead of us before our focus can move elsewhere."

Yercy nodded, nonplussed, then possibly relieved as those words convinced her to feel, if anything, a little less in the dark.

Underground Orchard

"Highchaw's celestial archives contain more data records than half of Ambright's collective knowledge amassed since the dawn of creation. It is used as a reference when evaluating how other realms might evolve from one culture to the next. Of course, Nev sometimes uses it to find new clothes."

- Pavilnean; a Highchaw scribe

Lola stopped midway through Sweven as a whisper leaked into her ears, startled equally by its familiar charm and the words themselves, both rooting down in her thoughts where they prodded emotions not touched in years. Resting on the emotions they caused would distract her, however. Such thoughts about Yercy's affection were thoughts needed elsewhere. The hospital's atmosphere had become dour lately.

The girl was connected to an IV unit filled with fentanyl, a drug used to combat pain, or more specifically, a drug administered on those whose life neared death. Drips of fluid fell from the bag and along plastic veins branching into a small, sleeping body. A doctor had exchanged her bandages. They'd been peeled off her skin like rotted bark, exposing the wounded flesh underneath. Faint voices told that Kronitare's last stage involved lacking energy paired by long fevers, both worsening each day.

Lola watched her counterpart's chest rise and fall, moving the sheets like a breathing mesa.

Nurses entered, checking vitals, and assuring their patient's well-being.

"Four weeks left, correct?" one asked. The other nodded.

"People say this room is haunted. Remember last week?"

"Don't get caught in rumors."

"Fine, but I do feel *something* alright."

"Terminals often give off those vibes. This child's truly been a fighter."

More faces came to acknowledge her and left uttering the same remarks about how life was short. They were colors smeared across Lola's peripheral vision as her thoughts moved by a different metronome of time. She stepped out to wander the hospital's passageways where people talked about old news that happened recently in their minds. A renowned building torn down. Someone's famous act spread across newspaper headlines. Strevenfall did away with newspapers once the radio hit, later improved when Typhame popularized aether-fueled circuitry. Several rooms murmured as people mourned beside lost relatives or friends, tightly creased mouths barricading pent-up emotions, tears filmed over pensive eyes. Stretchers rolled by, sometimes raced. Fathers carried sons atop shoulders. Mothers held their daughters' hands. Spouses bantered. People chatted around lobby tables.

In the girl's room again, colors stiffened the contours of Lola's frame as footsteps trickled in, contours locked upon realizing such colors belonged to Evelyn. The woman sat in the chair opposite to hers, the bed between them. Unease threatened her poise, a promise holding back what would have been another outburst. She breathed slowly instead and spoke. "You were the person who caused me the most pain in life, as in…you, you know?"

Evelyn's eyes were elsewhere.

"I'll never know if these visits mean something's changed you for the better. The years have convinced me you could never…well…change,

157

despite how much I wished you'd be someone who understood why my passion didn't need torture for it to prosper, me tortured along with it."

A pause. A shallow breath.

"Mother, you kept telling me I would like it in the end without once cheering me on. You picked out every mistake Valery had already drilled into me, about me doing better, performing better. I'd spend countless nights dreaming of a life without parents at all, then felt worse because I'd get even more lonely. Any interaction is better than aloneness, right? Yercy's play dates were the sole thing worth smiling about yet enjoying them was hard with practice scheduled afterwards. Everything was just a damn schedule, and everyone dragged me through it, forced me to act properly even if I couldn't stand upright because the depression had grown so unbearable, feeling sad, then feeling nothing."

Breathe. Shallow.

"Sometimes, I would just look around our living room, at Valery, you, Calvik, realizing I couldn't possibly escape. So many days people said things like, stand correctly or, face here, feet planted right, spine straight, toes straight, shoulders back, speak lady-like, hands braced, legs firm, waist perfectly aligned, wrong note, wrong measure, wrong play style, please, please, please, again and again and again and again. It all stuck with me growing up, alongside the physical abuse, of course. Gee, that sure did wonders beyond my childhood, after, well, after Yercy and I came of age, at least enough to finally end things after Brimothy stopped being afraid of you and stepped in. I actually believed these punishments were normal. Sitting in a closet room alone. Playing unclothed if yesterday's session had merely been average. Short cold showers, or none at all, or no meal, no outdoors, no sunlight; Valery's shock device that Calvik mindlessly used. I bet he was too satisfied with me playing unclothed to care about much else. I heard he was an astronomer until Aezial enlightened Strevenfall on Ambright's cosmology, ruining his career. The man likely thought I'd been born by accident, while he'd been drinking."

Shallow.

158

"Eventually, I realized more and more how depraved things were after it ended, and I lived alone. Parents don't torment their kids. Kids play, Mother. Kids have fun and grow and come into their own as the years give them insight, inspiration. I, however, didn't have that. Few befriended me while most kept their distance. I was constantly hungry, always punishing myself, depressed half the time, other times drunk, distraught after showering when the mirror reminded me of what being unclothed meant before I moved out. But hey, your daughter grew up into a 'charming little thing', as you put it. But get this, my first time at intimacy failed when I couldn't even stay naked long enough to enjoy it. But things were changing. Yercy showed me how to live, as did job friends, instructors, strangers even. Not you, though—never you. I started sleeping right, mostly. I started eating right."

Lola glared as the peafowl yawned, then calmed, knowing it was useless to point it out. "Perhaps what truly robbed my hope wasn't all that grief or anger, or what have you, but rather, that you seemed oblivious to what you were doing. Above all else, my pain fell on deaf ears. Much like now. You can't hear me no matter what I say." She rose heavily, pacing not two feet before Evelyn's unsuspecting stare. "So, let's cut the withered look, Mother, because it's a bit late to apologize, and your daughter won't need it anyhow. She's surviving this. Watch."

The peafowl left. Loud silence replaced her.

"When do I get a job?"

Lola turned. "Oh! You were awake."

The girl blinked tiredly. "What are other instructors like?"

She tried erasing her surprise, to no avail. "Well, it depends. Many turn out great."

"What does getting drunk do?"

"It loosens people up, makes them talk more, then not so much."

"And how does sex work?"

"Nice try."

"Okay, last question."

"Alright."

"Do you...like music?"

Lola's eyes widened by reflex, her shoulders raised slightly. "That's a silly question, right?"

The girl shrugged.

She replied, "Yes, absolutely," then added, "is what I'd say first."

"First? Then what would you say next?"

Her expression stilled, slowly, behind an idea that revealed itself like unfolding paper, before creasing at both ends. She hung there, eyes drifting away as if to flee the brain's tension.

Birds sang.

Trees danced.

Rainfall shimmered.

Young Yercy stopped at the entrance with a shrunken demeanor, regarding her companion who slept among tubes and dials beeping to an eldritch tempo. She approached, placing her hands on the girl's forearm as cannulas dripped fluid into pale skin. She was close to sobbing.

A journal landed beside her.

It read, *Have no worries.*

Yercy panned the room, knowing big Lola was around. "How much longer?"

The journal answered. *Three weeks, but we'll make our destination in less than two. May I write some questions?*

"Okay."

Thanks. Older Yercy wondered if I knew what happened after we would play onshore together, before Valery arrived. She looked troubled (though I can't really describe it) when I answered no. Could you tell me?

The nereid's body stiffened, regressed, and drooped, all carried like downcast weather.

Please.

160

She nodded. "No. It wasn't just when play times ended. It happened other times, lots, and lots of times."

What? Please tell me.

"I can't tell," her little voice cracked. "Da called it being sad because he would catch me pouting or crying, only those get better eventually, but not with me. The feeling feels different than getting cut by an urchin. I can't really say things about what happens, and I can't say things to her about it when we're playing. Who'd want a downer like me when she's already down on herself? She's always sad. She's sad when we build sandcastles, when we go hunting for shells, and she's sad even if we do nothing. Her parents are mean people, after all." Her voice cracked again as she leaned against the bedside, watching its patient slumber. "I can't imagine her going back to those people," she said, face half buried in the blankets. "I'm not sure how to bear it. Even my dad's frightened by them, so who's left to help?"

A ghost-like hand grazed the nereid's cheek. Having touched another, Lola's body twined with static and flicker pulling back towards the present, but she hardly cared. Enough had been said and felt.

Valtinespring appeared to be made solely for daylight's touch across its grain. Gold and canary meadows spanned well past the horizon, placed on flatland changed only by hills so gradual, they were nearly unseen. Lola gazed distantly as wheat grass swayed under the wind. Yercy knew she was exhausted, mentally exacerbated in part by their exchanged words at Sillstone; judgments shared with arguments, alterations, both leaving awkwardness.

Until Lola broke it. "How could I even like the violin?"

Yercy stared at her, puzzled.

"Stop the carriage."

"Whatever for?"

"Now."

161

Hooves silenced. Wheels locked. Lola hopped out and performed a song with six varied notes, twirling all the way. "Alright, how did I look? Happy? Joyed? Furious?"

"What? Why are you..." Yercy noticed her waver. "You look exhausted."

"Never mind that. Copper and I played this song named 'Foxtrot', and back then we must've been happy, right? I'm not now, though. Now it's the same feeling as always—always."

The nereid approached but Lola suddenly embraced her, and they stumbled back against the carriage where she was pinned against the door flap. "What's gotten into—"

"I don't feel worse," Lola panted, "but how could that be all? Surely playing with him couldn't make me feel the same as playing alone at night, and it's likewise anywhere else, on campus, or when I'm practicing alone...anywhere, everywhere."

"Please, let's get back on the wagon."

"I'm tired, so tired."

The few willows that grew in Valtinespring were prime camping grounds. Unable to drive, Lola instead took charge of mounting shelter, cooking, and cleaning. She eyed the roasted fruit and onions as if they moved.

Yercy watched her worriedly.

"As expected, Stalactite Cove is our final destination—should be reaching it within four days." Lola studied the map, squinting. "The landscape is said to be among the oldest in Strevenfall, a place of few inhabitants. The rivers there have a chemical makeup that can erase many kinds of viruses, like Kronitare, almost immediately."

"Garenham's given you quite the presentation voice."

At this, Lola exaggerated the tone. "As things were, Miss Rivitine, between my younger self's past and now, a vaccine was invented by Jamesel Gride, thus eliminating the need for this revered chemical water. Unfortunately, however, as things were, Miss Rivitine, such vaccines can only be administered before virus formation, not during, which explains why we can't use it now."

Yercy smiled somewhat. "After which, you're..."

"Helping to steer my younger self's future," Lola finished. "Crazy, I know."

"Crazy?"

"In a way, I suppose. Why, or how is it not?" She muttered something unheard, then, "Rather, how is it wrong? It can't be wrong to steer one's future when I know how gruesome it'll be, right?"

The nereid looked away.

"Right," she whispered. *Right.*

Dawn still shared the skies with the night as Lola rustled awake, restless from frenzied dreams since twilight. She held the violin and thought, distantly, what might happen if it were thrown against a tree, moments later placing the bow over her knee. Breaking either was absurd, obviously.

So, why did I have the idea?

She wobbled out of their tent where grass and grain brushed her ankles, her instrument held close. Clouds shaped the sun's rays, guiding her towards no place in particular. A field fire burned several miles off.

It's crazy.

Some grasshoppers chirped.

Why, or how is it not? It can't be wrong, right?

The moon was still rising.

What If I stop?

"Quiet!" Lola shrieked with blood-curdling vigor, frightening herself, because it was unlike the person she knew herself to be.

Why, or how is it not?

The sun hardly touched the hillside spotted not far ahead, the land slipping down towards what appeared like an underground hollow carved at its base. She had noted strange symbols dotting her map around here, perhaps of these very landforms, perhaps worth inspecting to distract these rambling, manic thoughts.

So, is it…escapism?

She entered the hollow carefully. Dust specks glinted while vines led into a wide, room-like area of trees, subterranean trees whose branches flourished with gold amber leaflets. Light gleamed from gaps spread across the canopy, greeting Lola as she wandered in with weary steps, her mind whirling. She stood among the orchard, mantled in the prospect of uncertainty that always seemed present besides other notions. What other notions? She tried recounting them, brushing fingers on the old maple trunks, catching a transience more benign than what came after. It sprouted briefly, shockingly mirthful, then left.

Lola stopped, confused.

This orchard reminded her of the abandoned haunts and cabins she once visited along Fervine's outer lands. She raised her bow and played, and she was there; sun shafts spreading through the windowless gapes of buildings left upon quiet fields, roadsides, shoals, a teenager performing serenades to hear how the notes rang against their old regal wood, how their rooms chambered sound, sometimes dancing, oftentimes seated in the largest room caked with dust drifting and reflecting noon's gorgeous glow, surrounded by vacant shelves, crumbled stairways, and lost heirlooms. Between each arrival she was ambling up street paths and thoroughfares, one arm feeling the breeze or grass touching her skin, the violin kept safely in hand. Days blurred. Raindrops glittered.

And then she was back, her bow down at her side, nearly mournful to be in the present as her memories overlapped, and when she regained focus, so did the fatigue that had taken root in her mind and body. She felt simultaneously loose and tight in her own skin. She felt as if to explode at any moment. Birds watched her stumble against the hillside when she left, witnessing her clarity finally run out.

Lola returned as Yercy watched the same field fire she'd noticed blaze in the distance.

The carriage rattled. The empty space softened from unworded noise as Lola's mind rang with heating thoughts.

It's crazy.

What If I stop?

Louder.

Louder.

Sounds swelling in her brain. Memories sewn with false pretenses seemingly real.

Disoriented, heavy with emotion, she could no longer ignore the presage given by her own lack of grip on reality. She would act on whatever impulse came next if it meant releasing the strain clawing at her thoughts, no matter what.

Windswept Sanity

"A change of mind and a change of heart are one in the same."

- Sprilla; a native of Jiken

Lola's mind slipped, not all at once, but little by little.

Minute by minute.

Hour by hour.

Day by day.

And she couldn't tell which increment of time moved faster, slower, set adrift in lucidity as ominous states of mind kept her in perpetual agitation; an origami city falling down. Faint markings upon the sidewalks, the buildings, and the towers, told that matters would eventually burn away. Her perception of the world changed whereas everything she saw, heard, and felt only aggravated the blaze in her mind, her body, while her words became less and less coherent, her thoughts less and less in order.

Weightless mass pinned her against the blankets, lifting long enough that she could probe their bags until Yercy clasped her shoulders asking desperately what was wrong.

"I have sleep paralysis, obviously," Lola said.

The nereid sighed. "What were you searching for?"

Tired, sheepish laughter.

"You're not making any sense."

"I know." Lola wasn't looking at Yercy. "I know."

Her lacking focus smeared the daylight hours into bands of light pulled past her eyes. Her breath tightened and curled sharply inwards, bursting outwards. She grabbed the carriage rail, panting.

But then night came again, stars interlaced with dreams of slanderous jeers racing through darkened red waters as cottonwood bodies lifelessly watched her struggle.

Day again; sun-stained clouds floating fast with prairie bugs clicking and the carriage rattling like an old jail cage.

Night. Restless stirring. Invisible weight holding her down. Her hands reaching for the luggage bags.

Daybreak. Nightfall. Dawn. Morning. Noon. Dawn. Twilight.

Dawn. Twilight

Dawn, twilight.

Dawn twilight.

"Lola!" Yercy steadied her. "You're more out of it than ever."

"Obviously, I have sleep paralysis."

People raced in when the girl's heart monitor flatlined. Its monotonous noise filled the room until their efforts recovered a heartbeat that before had been so faint as to elude the instrument's probes. Lola knelt at the bedside, brushing the child's face, kissing her forehead.

Amber grass peaked through Sweven's lagoon, replacing lily pads and flowers.

Amber grass flourished everywhere in present times. She pulled some and stared, then looked ahead. "A lagoon."

Yercy followed her near a vacant hillside.

Lola stopped at the water's edge. "You don't see it?"

"I don't see it."

"Oh, I must be insane, then." She waded several yards deep where turquoise filled around her knees. "Only fools believe in their own oasis, just another way the universe is refusing my choice. But we all know that'll never work, right? What reasons are there, anyway?"

"Lola..."

"None, precisely. That's why knowing you're against me feels horrible."

"Watching the child's health deteriorate has driven you mad, hasn't it?" Yercy closed their distance, leaving mere inches between them. "But this can't be the only thing that's bothering you. Please, let's just talk. We don't have to argue."

"Why? Think something's wrong with me?"

Wrong with me?

Wrong with me?

Wrong with me?

"Wrong with me?" Lola asked Evelyn in the hospital. "No, it's always been you. You got what Valery expected—a daughter whose forced-upon talent became the sole reason why Garenham accepted her, and why she excels everyone's forecasts."

She followed in the peafowl's trip back home, an apparition on the train, a back-seated ghost in her carriage, a phantom joining her among their living room's stale familiar aura of pipe smoke and crumpled music sheets, the front door closing. Calvik sat reading headlines. Both her parents were here.

Perfect.

Evelyn jumped as their window slammed shut, stifling the ocean's voice. Tension-filled ambiance stopped Calvik's approach to check it.

Several minutes passed.

The wall clock hushed and the phonograph player switched on, its sparkling tune by a quartet of singers. Disembodied movement approached as they fearfully huddled in the living room's center. Window drapes pulled, floors creaked, closer, a paper moved, lights flickered, closer.

Silence rang.

Longer.

Longer, closer, and longer still.

Suddenly, noise thundered when brass and wood crashed into porcelain, spraying shards like shrapnel, their phonograph having been flung towards a plate cabinet. Cracked melodies, broken lyrics hummed along as Calvik tried escaping only to find every door jammed from the outside. Evelyn dashed upstairs in search of the breach alarm. She looked utterly panicked, hysterical, stumbling through dark rooms like a beaten house cat. A toppled wardrobe scared her back, terrified, then agonized when a flower vase struck from behind and plunged the woman downstairs in a thudding heap of cries and bruises.

Calvik helped up his wife who now limped with a battered leg bleeding from its kneecap. The couple hobbled to the only room left unhaunted—their kitchen. Of course, they hadn't fled downstairs to the basement yet. The irony was gorgeous. Evelyn's eyes screamed what she choked on, pain, terror, jolts sputtering down her arms as if shocked with electric steel.

Gorgeous.

A light bulb died.

Drawers fell.

Evelyn yelped when her hand pressed on a glowing stove top that was previously off. More chaos stirred as the peafowl's face twisted, turning pale and full of fear, outright fear piercing through her skin, deeper into bone, then out again past the eyes.

But this distracted Lola from Calvik. He tore open a flour bag and threw its contents with panic in his face, flailing wildly. White dust fell atop a massless shape making footprints as it jumped back in surprise, but he'd already drawn a carving fork and moved, jabbing towards this creature before escape was possible.

Silent cries. Blood trickled.

Calvik advanced and pushed the creature back towards a wall with maddened strikes tearing unseen fabric. Crimson trailed from wounds suspended like blood-stained mobiles. The creature was pinned, the man jabbing, again and again until the creature lunged forth before his red-slicked steel dealt another blow, touching the man's arm. A flicker faded, then vanished, nothing.

Lola squeezed cloth against her wounds while biting off gauze strips, sweating with lightheaded fatigue. Four cuts in total, two on her abdomen, one above her breasts, the other drawn across her temple.

Restless stirring. Invisible weight holding her down. Lola wrenched awake and crawled for the luggage bags, pulling back clothes, navigation tools, at last finding a knife that was cold to the touch. Holding the silvery glint tight against her chest, she turned, as if facing a criminal, when a soft voice beckoned from behind.

Yercy watched the knife in Lola's possession, her hands sliding cautiously down Lola's shoulders, arms, over Lola's own hands as they shivered, until they loosened, the knife relinquished.

"You wouldn't believe why I'm acting like this," Lola shrugged. "It's too dramatic."

"I'd believe anything now," said Yercy.

She replied with wry humor. "Is that a challenge? I've been hallucinating Sweven in the form of bits and fragments, sometimes a strange white building where none should be, others with water collected in places stranger still, hence the lagoon incident six days ago. The dreamworld's been not so much a dream, Rivitine. Telling if I'm dreaming at all wanes my focus even more. A good poke on my arm ought to set me right, right?"

"Six days? The lagoon was half that time ago."

"I'll be safe, promise!" She lunged tiredly for the knife only to slump across Yercy's leg, sleeping.

Seconds blew over hours over days and around like violent winds. Pale blank towers pierced the meadow's face. An overflowing river drowned nearby valleys. During eventide, Lola stood among the wide pastures to recite ephemeral joy killed by rue, frustrated, then angry. The tremolo's rapid waver buckled with more memories pressed like hot brands across her brain.

It was nighttime. She thrashed awake and ran across the midnight hills, wounded, directionless, stopping at a nonexistent rill, at fake architecture. She plunged through another lagoon and allowed its depth to drag her down, soak her dress with unreal water.

They tortured me.

I'm torturing me.

But I promised.

What of it?

What if I proceed?

"I'll be here," she said in Valery's doll room, visiting again. "I'll be helping."

But I'll be here.

The past seldom called now as her counterpart's unconscious hours drew more over daylight, so she used Tinman Tom's alarm function to play "Hummingbird's Verse" every noon and evening. The girl's breath was shallow, raspy, passing through her mouth like wind-spooled spirits aimed to leave their home. Evelyn hadn't returned recently even though she'd love to skin her alive. Hospitals held plenty of tools, scalpels, scissors. She imagined using a few, their sharpest ends rammed into the peafowl's belly.

Lola sat against the wall, appalled by her thoughts, yet wanting them more.

…Want.

What do I want?

A redeemed childhood, reconciled.

To what extent?

"Until there's closure." She stood amid the hospital's gardens outside, remembering when the girl had capered between its flowers. "I'll be with her."

You are her.

From my past.

171

Of which cannot change the present.

Winds blew as Valtinspring revealed its starkest vibrancy, plains of gold canary shifted to amber, then orange, vermilion, at last landing on red, rich scarlet spread like molten pigment overland, stretched beyond Strevenfall's skyline. Lola referenced their map.

Valtinspring: Robin's Blanket.

But this clashed with her illusionary mindscape, lagoons gathered between hills, spires and buildings strewn like dead foreign bodies. Scarlet. Turquoise. Ivory. All joined without pretense or subtlety, near-overwhelming scenery constructed in part by unbridled imagination.

She approached the nearest spire, drifted through its mouth, and explored darkened rooms mazed like an abstract puzzle. Most held nothing, others containing fragments of furniture, lone chairs, tables, things stranger still, a phonograph, papers, knives, spilled ink. A doll's dismembered head lay in blood, birds stapled on walls.

Dazed, verging on complete delirium, she paused to write a journal entry.

And Yercy witnessed her stand midair, a ghost, a poltergeist held aloft by invisible floors, caught in past transgressions, one who rose from smoldering covers of which dreams had set aflame. The nereid weighed if intervening now would lighten matters or make them worse, or if it would even make a difference now. "What do you see?" she called.

No reply, invisible walls blocking the sound.

Familiar, Lola thought, frightened. The grass whistled underfoot.

You know what's inevitable. This outcome. These omens.

Just look around, at yourself, and within.

"Naw...me?" She tripped languidly, falling face first. "Not a chance, bud."

You can't last forever.

I've suffered worse.

So you tolerate this as well?

Notions burned.

Flared.

What nonsense.

Sweven changed again, water floored by sea grass varnished red, buildings bleeding with the color. Lola paced raggedly further and further across the dreamworld, closer to where the water fell off and disappeared. Did she hate what she was doing? Did she hate *herself* for what she was doing?

Doing? What exactly am I...doing?

The water tugged her legs...

Where did I get these...motives?

...pulled her out...

I'd love to sleep now.

...near Sweven's ledge...

Just five minutes

...and over...

Whoops, tripped again.

Aqueous wind howled during the freefall, five seconds, ten.

Her body struck the ground with bone-pulverizing force as it landed in the shallow water, but there was no pain, nothing broken. Slovenly clothes soaked with something dead. Hair splayed like raven feathers.

At first, Lola wasn't moving. Then, with apathetic slowness, she rose on all fours, head heavy with the rush of impact felt without the damage. She stood shakily in the darkness that was broken only by a red, faded glow—a curdling, omnipresent aura. Sweven's enclave hovered from what seemed like miles above. She scanned the scenery as something metallic spurred her tongue, before realizing the familiar airborne tang of something rancid.

...Rancid.

Doused in blood, she stumbled several yards out, then more, indeed finding no end to it as her breath tightened, arms folded taut with her nails dug below her rib cage. A glance back confirmed at least some distance from the now smaller enclave, be it hardly.

But it wasn't long until the first mounds of bodies loomed into view, cloth skins and hard plastic eyes reflecting back their trespasser, or maybe their heiress.

Then, the voices started churning; an abrasive chorus of echoes reminding her of times had in despondency.

Lola stood hard against it, fragile yet resolute as her eyes raised to glare sharply back, both scared and enraged. Perhaps a faint smile teased her mouth, murder tickling her lips. "No, this is perfect," she muttered wearily. "I have been expecting my nightmare, and now, here you are."

She pulled the knife from her sundress, fingers creased around its hilt. Shaking?

"Just stay there. Don't. Move."

All means are necessary.

Even this.

Even, this.

There was a break............

.....................in thought.

And Lola charged screaming, feet splashing through blood as she neared the closest mound and plunged her knife through a rag doll's stomach, piercing through its spine...its spine. She reared to another doll and severed the arm, reared again, a different face slashed ear to ear, again, a body sawed in half, her throat raw from bellows of anger.

Again.

Again.

The furor ceased, eventually. These bodies were heavy, not so much filled with cotton or kapok wool. Instead, mottled entrails soused her blade, gore and tendons sliding down its edge, slipping off to float amid the sea of red. She looked over. A doll's gash bled. Another's rib cage was torn. Flesh held within fabric. Small bodies filled of which filled her. Bones weaved between organs.

Still, the voices burned, and she wobbled back, doused in startled exhaustion, feeling sick. Her stomach knotted at the sight of their own stomachs mauled, intestines spilled over limbs and dead faces.

Lola quivered, the knife pressed along her forearm.

Wake up! Please, wake up!

Her next thought struggled for calm, failing. The one after sought meaning.

I can't be deterred...not now.

She looked on with uncertainty at first, then her eyes narrowed, knowing the voices had no end unless it was forced upon them. She deserved to let go, to finally snap if it meant gaining some sense of release, some sense of control, stopping this carousel before the damage proved irreversible.

I've already gone too far.

She attacked the dolls again. The knife, a soaked blur of crimson, tore through skin and tissue until the difference in either seemed meaningless. Perhaps Lola's cries would have remained audible if someone had watched from the enclave's ledge as it loomed over her like an eclipse. She climbed up the piles of small bodies and struck out with both hands gripping the knife handle. Lamed dolls were thrown aside to expose the ones underneath, but sometimes, hands alone sufficed in tearing them apart.

Everything lost form to her, strangely, maybe due to adrenaline, or faintness numbing the body. Her sounds and movements reduced to echoes, far-off explosions leaving just two things in focus—the voices and her—one prodding the other like spurs to an animal's side. She allowed this marriage, fearfully, because it simplified what would've otherwise been yet another vague question. How did the nightmare and Sweven merge together?

But in truth, Lola knew, or at least the answer dawned gradually as she gouged body after body, arms, legs rolling aside, not daring to stop and think, not letting it hit.

Is it...escapism?

175

"Yes!" Lola cried. "Shut up! Shut up!"

Confessing it merely revealed the answer more so than before, however, like a flame held against her soul.

She didn't know how much time passed, what time was anymore, or when her chaos slowed as a thought echoed through it.

I've already gone too far.

She caught her reflection in the sea of gore, black hair over bloodshot eyes, her skin splattered from butchery. She was on all fours, indeed like an animal, staring at it.

Look around, at yourself, and within.

She leaned back, face tilted up, eyes shut, then she rose, the sea littered with carnage, and her expression now calmed with acceptance.

"Within," she whispered, the knife dropping. "Within me."

What if I stop?

And for once, there was no objection.

Lady Cosmos

"... The stars have arrived and we're moving on to the next phase of ourselves, treading through the vastness in search of a place to watch the comets race. Time is a force we can bend with the gravity emitted by the music we make. An obsession with the past is what ties you down like a tether, while a separation would bring you out into the great unknown. Constellations told of a world beyond the frosted house and forestland, but the fear in your bones collides with an aching yearn for closure. I will be shapeless in the end, a child figment of light."

- "Hummingbird's Verse"; lyrics part 3

Crystals snowed from a mythic atmosphere miles away, glints of diamond catching sun as they drifted upon Robin's Blanket to embellish its tapestry spread beyond the horizon's edge. They drifted over lonesome trees and prairieland swallowed by scarlet grass, under clouds and valley panoramas swathed in late-morning glow.

They drifted near Lola, who stood atop a hillside overlooking the world whose barrier between reality and not had dissipated. Lagoons pooled amid ivory domes and towers strewn overland, alien designs dreamed from an orphic, damaged mind.

Her mind, as the recent epiphany indicated, had not been revealed to anyone, yet.

She returned to the carriage parked downhill. Yercy sat against its wheel, legs curled, arms wrapped around them.

"Never knew I had it in me," said Lola, her words trailing off.

Yercy blinked. "At first, I couldn't even tell it was you."

"Me neither."

"You woke up covered in blood that just...appeared, everywhere, and not just blood."

"There's no need describing it. We both already know."

"So, what now?"

"Now, a different choice urges me to no end, at least I think so. It's a choice that was already available to me but one I've been ignoring all along."

Yercy regarded the dress Lola had discarded for fresh clothes; a claret-soaked phantom. "A different choice...as in, one worth taking? Because ignoring what all this time traveling has done to you is suicide now. *Literally*, suicide. But I can tell you're still weighing the options. Why? Surely that hellish world finally proved—"

"Hey."

"—what'll happen if—"

"Hey! Let's just...go, alright?" A diamond settled on Lola's palm. "The bizarre weather's not part of my dreamworld. Stalactite Cove mustn't be too far."

They resumed the trail now leveled to ruts while emotion's gravity nulled any would-be dialogue. Their surroundings were mute, however, as if yielding for words or musical reverie, or coalesced thought. A birdless sky watched Lola, whose memory explored the answer, learning its shape like a new constellation. She'd regretfully resisted her own objections. The present's inertia focused solely on what was here, more so than before.

And what's here, she thought, *is me, focused elsewhere.*

Valtinespring hushed its parting with tapestry soothed and swallowed by change yet again, the scarlet fanned, faded, then gone completely. Their carriage rattled over jagged topography, over slabs and shards prickling under the wheels where no path remained. Sunlight refracted off translucent terrain—a land made of crystals layered across the scenery like armor. Skies turned silver-white. Hills turned into clustered, translucent pillars.

Their map read, *Stalactite Cove: The Pearl Plains.*

Niveous, crystallized dust fell in greater strength now as temperatures cooled. But Yercy seemed impervious to it, instead wrapped in docile silence.

…Is me, pushing her away.

"Stop our carriage."

The carriage stopped. Lola climbed onto its roof with scrambled footing, offering down a hand. Yercy followed despite her better judgment, because something had moved, something realigned in her companion's demeanor. They both stood shakily on the carriage latticework, but they were standing nonetheless.

"What's this about?" Yercy wobbled to stay upright.

"A testimony," Lola replied, "because my recent comedown has left insight that I'd normally just ignore, but not this time. Here, just summarize what's around us…Strevenfall's most bizarre region, right? Stalactite Cove. Now imagine Strevenfall's most bizarre region joined with Sweven's."

"I've tried before. It's overwhelming."

"Yes, overwhelming." She was breathless somehow. "And truthfully, I've been overwhelmed long before my past manifested. 'Hummingbird's Verse' merely framed the situation with more, well, let's say visual flare, and along the way came this idea of Sweven being a world separate from me when, really, it's one I created."

The nereid turned, perplexed.

"Which would have been obvious given a healthier mindset, but that's just it. Sweven has always lived inside me because…it's *my* headspace, only

179

now granted form by a song that, when played, pulls me from the present time to explore this headspace. And I've fallen down the worst of it lately...the worst of me."

"But if Sweven is actually your mind—who's the child?"

"Same as always. After all, what is the past if not memories transpired? And what's the future if not memories placed ahead?"

Yercy blinked, taken aback. "That's...quite the motto. So, do plans about her remain, or, what? What are you implying?"

Lola shrugged.

"And why did we climb up here?"

Lola shrugged again, smiling.

Gargantuan pillars of clear tourmaline gemstones rose ahead as they traveled further, cylindrical monoliths spanning miles wide with heights piercing the clouds like scepters. All other things were small in comparison, only nothing else thrived, no flora, no fauna, just their carriage, a tiny speck drawn towards landscape seemingly forged by celestial giants.

Stalactite Cove: Star Sanctuary.

No subtleness.

No gradual elevation.

And there were no signs of native citizenry until, once they'd neared the frontmost pillar, four pallid figures approached, four children, four little moon sylphs with white clothes and black stockings matched by curious eyes. Yercy laughed as one climbed aboard whilst the others pointed onward saying, "Follow us!" or "Astrid loves travelers!"

They followed and found themselves swallowed in crystalline inscape, stepping through the pillar's entry that spilled into myriads of grand rooms and tenements woven with halls, an elaborate mansion, masterfully designed.

Lola was helped to a chair when she became dizzy.

"How goes it?" asked Yercy.

She smirked. "Running on fumes."

Around them were chairs and tables and decor constructed out of translucent rock, even the air vents and walls, the doors and the very fastenings holding it all together. Everything was quartz. Everything refracted light and shimmered, the floors above partly visible through the ceiling.

"I can hardly believe I dragged us here," Lola whispered. "I'm sorry."

Yercy grinned. "Don't be. It's a nice place."

"Still bantering after all the times I've yelled at you, after all my choices. You're crazy putting up with me."

A pause, then, "I'll put up with you, no matter the choice."

Someone approached down the gemstone stairway, a young moon sylph maiden bringing jeweled chains and ornaments swinging with her movements. "Apologies for my delay!" she called. "We seldom have guests and I'm still a novice at proper welcoming procedures!"

Embellishments were gifted equally by the maiden who now curtsied with practiced yet rudimentary flare, lifting her smooth ivory garb to expose black leggings underneath, traditional clothes perhaps. The gesture's casual style contrasted with the hard rigid scenery, as if it somehow didn't belong in such a place. It was welcoming, yes, but guarded, as seen when her posture straightened afterwards; heedful, somewhat prim.

The nereid studied her new pendants.

Lola did not. "Astrid, right?"

"Stalactite Cove's biannual groundskeeper," Astrid nodded. "Such a tired physique implies that you're here on critical matters. Please tell."

Lola elaborated on her cause, the odyssey of mindscapes crafted by a magic song, of bridged timelines plagued by a narrative illness, feeling lightheaded, but managed to finish stating her case.

Astrid caught the certitude in Lola's voice, her eyes obscured by snowy hair so that no one realized how awed they were. Awed, and troubled. "Our dripstone caves bare many tonics," she explained, "including those that erase terminal viruses like Kronitare. However, less come here for those reasons as traditional medicines evolve. Most clients nowadays arrive either to work in peace or meditate. That being said, your predicament is...extraordinary, delicate...dangerous."

Yercy caught a glimpse of the maiden's lips tightening.

They were led to a room of skewed architecture, of walls made from huge, mirrored gem shards angled to break one's reflection many times over. Lola stood near the center. Her body split among countless ways, exposing every detail: unkempt hair, clotted wounds—and those since ignored: trembling thighs, paled skin, and panting breath.

"Please, regard the syndromes ailing you," Astrid said, standing aside with Yercy. "I've more than half a mind to call the paramedics right now. No human endures this much sleep deprivation without lasting effects."

Lola frowned. "No, really?"

"Miss Pern, sarcasm is hardly appropriate. My gem shards reveal a woman whose health deteriorates so long as her voyage lengthens. Permitting you into the caverns would fall at the expense of my client's safety. As a groundskeeper, I must deny your request."

"What?" Yercy gasped. "But the child's sickness adds to Lola's!"

Astrid ignored her. "I'm sure you understand."

"Yercy tells the truth," said Lola. "Restoring my counterpart's well-being comes first."

"Does it? Or perhaps your condition reflects one's inability to move on. Perhaps the reason behind your infirmity stems from excessive time travel, excessive trips visiting the child who, by what I hear, is a rogue memory of the past."

"I'm not leaving without a cure!"

"And what's to happen afterwards, Miss Pern, after the child is saved?"

No reply; a wish caught between hemispheres.

"Please don't make us turn back after all we've—" Yercy paused, thinking. "We'll absolutely refuse any medical help until the cure is gathered, and if we turn back, her condition will plummet even more. Lola's health rides on *your* decision."

Astrid's snow-like gaze narrowed, her arms crossed.

"Would begging suffice?" Lola finished, and her panting was audible through the following silence, silence that lingered, tight, like a turmoil at bay.

"Fine, I'll...deliberate overnight." Astrid regarded Lola quite strangely now. "But only because I question what really ails you, time travel or otherwise." Her expression finally softened. "If by chance you're granted access, give a deadline of the child's remaining life span."

"Five days," Yercy replied, because Lola was faint. "However, we ought to have the cure tomorrow. Its effects have a short delay."

"Very well. Tonight's accommodations require no payment. Please, rest."

The guest rooms swam with luxury, resembling shrunken mansions, white quartz tables and floors and bathrooms, while the windows overlooked Strevenfall, the view sprawling for miles. Lola chose the nearest room and would've collapsed if Yercy hadn't helped her into bed. She was feverish, sweating.

Diamonds snowed outside. A dead bird fell on the nightstand.

Muted footsteps: Yercy was toting up their belongings.

A delicate noise: The breeze flying.

She slept—until midnight loomed—then roused somewhat refreshed. Yercy faced her from the opposite bed, dreaming, stirring as Lola rustled off the mattress to where her toes touched upon the cold, polished floor. She moved carefully, and was gone.

Gone to explore crystalline architecture now mellowed with afterdark, its brilliance tamed, but still very much alien. Glass-like chandeliers hung from ceilings high, ceilings that reached across vast corridors lined with empty rooms, towering over the furniture and bookshelves, while the walls reflected the drifter passing near them.

The drifter stopped at a colonnade. Moonlight glowed between pillars placed widely apart, resembling an open balcony that seemed to go on forever overground. Lola, small in comparison, stood amid two pillars and played her violin. Sandals moved across the floor, an arm swayed to starry skies, soft moments framed years prior. But something had changed.

"What are you remembering?"

She turned to where Astrid sat patiently near the back wall and frowned. "You've been watching me this whole time?"

Astrid remained in full lotus, mute, moonlight streaking across her eyes whose curiosity somewhat mirrored the children's. She blinked expectantly.

Lola decided to answer. "I remember exploring Fervine's outer lands for the sake of peace and quiet, much like now. Yercy calls it escapism."

"But that's not what *you'd* call it, correct?"

"Please, do I really need someone prying into my psyche now? The week's already been too much. Shouldn't you have been asleep hours ago?"

"Moon sylphs are a nocturnal lot."

"Nocturnal." Lola chuckled. "Yes. Yes of course."

Astrid rose daintily, and boldly approached the colonnade's edge as if drawn there by design. "Come with me."

Where? Lola couldn't ask out loud, instead watching the maiden's shoulder blades glow with energy; white vaporous light stretched into wing-shaped appendages. She'd forgotten that sylphs could fly. Her bow dropped. It was breathtaking.

"On the top floor lies a showpiece you may recognize," Astrid answered her thought, "but it's only accessible through flying. I can bring us there."

Lola agreed, agreed to take her hand, locking arms with her wrist to wrist, agreed to step off the ledge where night's cool air waited, to then rise as she did, all because something had pulled between them, perhaps a common respect, or maybe it was the freedom that oftentimes formed between strangers who had a lot on their minds. And now she floated freely under Strevenfall's stars where the air whistled and fear twined with ecstasy. Astrid's strength was more than what her appearance let on. They spiraled up the pillar with ease, arriving at its topmost floor elevated so high that clouds roamed beneath, an open-air patio smoothed to a reflective shine.

While Astrid flew back down to fetch her violin, Lola walked in a slow circle around the platform's focal point—a magnificent piano—a masterpiece of clear crystal construction that not only showed off all its inner regalia but allowed the moonlight to bounce and reflect off the keys, hammers, and strings.

"Look familiar?" Astrid asked upon returning.

"Nebula's Concert Grande," Lola nodded. "Sage Meisu spent years building it from scratch. It was used in the Noceur Orchestra."

"And donated to us when Meisu passed away." The maiden stepped aside and curtsied.

"Oh, I couldn't possibly—"

"Gone on. Take the seat."

Swallowing, Lola sat to perform a quick melody. This jewel was tuned with utter perfection.

"Good, now hop off and choose from Garenham's duet catalog. You'll play secondary while I'm dominant." Astrid's hands hovered above the keys. "Or better yet—just play whatever comes to mind. I'll fill in the gaps."

We're playing? But again, her thoughts drifted away. She began blindly, catching rhythm and verve and her feet moved across the belvedere, dress swaying. The maiden's chord weaved as background ambiance granting room for experimentation. They harmonized; resonance splayed across the notes like a silver wave. Astrid watched her play with calm self-indulgence, as if nothing mattered except the clouds and stars.

Astrid stopped, then stood, stretching her arms. "Now would you call our duet escapism? If so, I must have gotten the wrong impression about music."

"I played alone before," said Lola.

"The difference eludes me, Miss Pern."

She laughed with pain behind her eyes, then slowed, stopping. "You think I'd still get this far with music, given a better childhood, and different parents?"

"Well, who loved music first? You or them?"

They stood abreast, conversing under a star-drenched canopy while the comets raced, and the moon lingered high into morning's first hour. Astrid was eighteen, knew basic magecraft, and had been chaired for groundskeeping several months prior. Her interests hopped from painting, piano, and teaching new acolytes, which explained the children. Lola was twenty-two, could play several instruments, and had been chosen among Garenham's finest several years prior. Her interests hopped from dancing, music, and piloting boats, which explained her sea legs. Stalactite Cove received few visitors during springtide's end. Most favored the outdoors over an artist's retreat where silent clouds veiled the daylight's weather. These clouds always parted by night, however, yielding room for Strevenfall skygazing.

Astrid finished saying that before crossing her arms. "You know how to mend the time travel curse, don't you?"

Lola's mouth tightened, but there was no use in arguing. "Yes. At least, I know where it's solved anyway. 'Hummingbird's Verse' once had lyrics that can still be sought after within Garenham's archives. The answer is certainly there."

"Ah, so this was all a matter of closure to begin with. Personal vindication."

Vindication, repeated in her mind.

"You are a curious individual, Miss Pern."

Closure, echoed across her thoughts.

...Closure.

Ashen light filtered through the windows and balconies and warmed the pillar's heart. Noon had nearly struck when a sylph child stopped by their room to announce Astrid's approval. Relief swelled through Lola, feeling it like a sign of things to come. She faced the bathroom mirror, nails biting her palms, tighter, tighter, then loosening, then again, again, again.

Not much longer, Pern.

She eyed Yercy waiting at the door.

Not much longer.

They were escorted down numerous flights of stairs, down multiple floors, past glistening statues, beneath glittering chandeliers, on and on until the sunlight waned, then until it was gone completely. Wall lamps guided them towards a cavern's mouth carved through the hall. Beside the entrance were tables littered with topographical diagrams, and beside those, Astrid stood, studying a map whilst leaning on one foot, the other fidgeting.

"Something amiss?" Yercy asked.

The map lowered. "No, just checking Stalactite Cove's layout before our departure. I've not been a groundskeeper long enough to know it by heart."

"We can't thank you enough," said Lola.

"Consider us friends, Miss Pern. Last night's performance was gratifying."

A placard posted above the cavern entrance read, *Stalactite Cove: Tonic Archive.*

It was a maw that swallowed galaxies. Dripstone teeth crowned the ceiling while blades of crystal shot from below, and below they traveled, taking the path woven carefully throughout this underground world coated with stars, soft glints of light, some falling from the roof where they fell into the basins, the pools, the ponds.

Water, Lola thought. *Mineral water.*

Their footfalls echoed well into the cavern's hollows, its many stalactite chambers that, upon closer observation, varied by color, by type. Closer still, and she noticed that each tooth was labeled with waterproof paper wrapped around them. Everything was cataloged, everything accounted for.

"Each mineral cluster yields different tonics and medicines." Astrid waved about. "The water dripping from these clusters holds their respective remedies in a distilled form, ideal for consumption or intravascular means. Kronitare's own remedy shouldn't be too far. Chamber number forty-one. Two miles straight, third left, second right."

"Was Dr. Kavlador truly the first to discover Kronitare's antidote in Stalactite Cove?" asked Lola. "He *is* the man I researched before leaving Garenham."

"A question better aimed at historians. I know several apothecaries who make rounds here for research purposes, but none whose last name is Kelvador. It sounds Eatherian. His parents must have hailed from the realm of Hobe."

The path narrowed into a capillary vein carved between pools set aglow with aether. Another chamber waited at its end, a small dome with stalactites belting the perimeter, flower stones placed evenly therein. And there it was. Several clusters spiked out of the farthest corner, labeled 'Triveriandide4199'. Kronitare's antidote.

Lola knelt before them, watching vibrant tears trickle down their sides, falling to the ground in a slow, methodical tempo.

Yercy knelt beside her. "We're here."

"Yes," Lola whispered. "We're finally here."

Astrid knelt opposite as the tears fell between them. It suddenly occurred to Lola that Valery had also been a moon sylph. The maiden's cloud-hazel eyes, moon-colored skin, and silver-white hair, all coalesced into an appearance that now seemed familiar. Perhaps her old instructor had appeared likewise during her adolescence, and perhaps, around then, she'd no desire to exploit those with musical verve. Could matters have been different under changed circumstances? If events were swapped, realigned, altered?

Her thoughts floated as the moon sylph pushed a bowl underneath the dripstone's weeping face, droplets falling, landing, filling slowly.

She glanced at Yercy sidelong.

I know you're worried sick about me...

Falling.

...terrified of what happened...

Landing.

...maybe afterwards, we can just...

Filling.

...well, after things...change.

There was no objection.

There was quietude in the hours drawn ahead, after the bowl filled with sparkling water, once they'd left the tonic archive, and Astrid retreated elsewhere to ready the cure. Clouds brightened as noontide shone above them. Relief had possibly never felt this strange before, minutes lapped together as Lola peered over Strevenfall from between the colonnade's pillars, waiting, wondering, the nereid beside her, and behind her, an odyssey.

Almost, almost behind.

"Guess now that depends on me, right?" she murmured.

Yercy nodded.

"I can hardly distinguish what's real and not. Sweven has pretty much joined with the real world at this point...It's just, my mind...all around us, everywhere. When we first arrived here, I thought Stalactite Cove was part of the dream, Astrid too. Some things look similar to fiction, don't they?" She lay back, sprawled across the floor, crystal flecks landing on her face. "Or perhaps there's little difference."

Thoughts lifted, bending through memories, people, past and present, a tempest, a tethered wistfulness wound with less tension. The impression of last night's musical reverie felt different now, as if predetermined sadness was itself fiction, because, looking back, she'd been happy. Tired, yet happy, perhaps. So, what about the other instances of that, of going out to play under the night's roof?

"The difference eludes me, Miss Pern," the maiden had said.

"Yes, you're bitter!" Yercy had claimed.

Yes, she thought now, *bitter towards the past, and so, towards those who I shared it with. Not just those responsible for its chaos, but everyone.*

...Including you.

Astrid returned, a small silicon pouch nursed in her palms. Its contents resembled stars teeming within finite space, tiny glimmers of white winking at Lola as the moon sylph gave her the item, the treasure, the completed purpose for this journey across Strevenfall, across time.

And now, here it was, resting on her hands, exchanged through simple weight and physical being, a wordless breath held in response. Pliable. Innocent. A sure-felt manifestation of her travels. She thought about crying, really, if not to ease the emotion's onset. Yercy cupped her shoulder, lightly, while the maiden stood aside, allowing stillness to blend with the moment's gravity.

Snow diamonds fell around them.

Skies silver-bright.

Stalactite Cove glistening with all manner of crystal majesty.

Breathe.

Relax.

Breathe

"Very well," said Lola, "I've made my choice."

A Break in the Nebula

"… A soft yellow light filtered out from an open window on the last floor of the keep. Ealdhelm grabbed the window ledge and looked into the bedroom. A thin man sat at a long wooden desk, his back to Ealdhelm. He stooped over his writing, a pen scraping across the paper in short, hurried strokes. He muttered the words as they came…"

- The Droodpike Parables VI

Velvet-soft light shimmered through the doorway's aperture.

Commotion rumbled soft and smooth beyond quiet walls.

Voices like a song emitted by distant stars.

The girl's vision had fogged recently; muted colors on whitened irises. Instinctively, she'd blink in hopes of quelling the noise, a keen hurried motion, to no avail. White veils spoke of the virus's effects on retinal veins. Her counterpart once explained it using simpler terms. Long, long dreams craned like a moonbow across minutes, hours, until a sunburst thought would wake her with the heart monitor's tempo fading,

…fading

…fading

…fading.

...into an echo haunted by its own number. Everything was silent, strangely—peaceful?—a celestial tide never to rise again. How many waves crawled ashore? The heart monitor continued beeping.

62...

    61...

        60...

She awakened from another dream, breath ragged, her appetite flown. The ceiling twirled without motion. Frayed, chime-like sounds jingled faraway. Every stir seemed equal parts light and heavy, louder, bed sheets sliding, the pillow crinkling as she watched where shadows bent about the room's corners and how light played with them, at great soundlessness carried over the drywall. It looked so important now.

Colors changed, a figure blurred near the door frame, lithe and beautiful and kneeling at her bedside. Her other half never failed to visit when no one else did. A hand nestled on her forehead, and for a second all grieved notions were secondary behind the softness pulling them back. A few patient moments elapsed between this gesture and when the hand moved finally down to her wrist, resting there. It was anchorage, amity's refuge when fear proved thickest. A connection. A confidant.

Now, big Lola spoke. The girl's spirits lifted, slow, calm, and decompressed. It was the stuff of fairy tales, of a journey through crystal rooms and sparkling caverns, a cure gathered, now dripping through her veins like magic. She felt weightless, weakness muttering farewell despite the magic's delay, already smiling, simply glad and looking up knowing this drywall wouldn't last much longer.

I'm leaving...leaving.

A lengthened pause, big Lola's hand tightening until blood was felt pulsing through the grip, before it loosened. Her voice reached again, slow and solemn. It pulled the girl down from her worry and discontent, but landed her someplace different, unfamiliar. Her breath quickened, quivering through a mouth hung open as if to speak in reply, but whose lips trembled.

When her counterpart finished speaking, nothing remained but a broken promise, the air between them punctuated by the heart monitor's tempo reading sixty, set to rise regardless of the unfallen tears that glazed over the girl's eyes now. They pooled at the corners and spilled over. She cried mutely, chest fluttering. Bedman Berry wrinkled when Lola settled next to her. Lola embraced her, kissed her cheek, her forehead, and then allowed her to fall asleep.

A flicker.

A pulse.

A weight lifted from the bed sheets. One passenger remained, and soon, merely one would ever be.

Velvet light passed through the doorway's aperture.

Commotion rumbled soft and smooth beyond quiet walls.

Notions like a song emitted by nearby stars.

Lola swayed dizzily as she entered the girl's hospital room, flushed from traveling across Sweven yet again, her health waned, but the girl's health mattered more now. It mattered to both of them. She exchanged the IV bag for Kronitare's tonic, breathlessly fervent, and finally, seated near the bed where its passenger watched with cloud-covered eyes. Their blithe expressions mirrored, mostly, a kinship set ajar now as one smile faded. Lola brushed the girl's forehead, and for a second all grieved notions were secondary to the softness pulling them back. A few patient moments slipped by between this gesture and when it proceeded down to her wrist, stopping there. It was protection, amity's refuge when fear was at its worst. A connection. A confidant. A reason to separate.

Come on Pern. Speak up.

"Listen, I've come for other reasons, too," she began. "There's no good time to tell you this, so I'll tell you now...

...My desire came from a place of hurting, honestly..."

"...we mustn't continue, not like this..."

"...I can't help us otherwise..."

"…please, please understand…"

I'm leaving…leaving.

"…Sweven would expand to no end…"

"…merging with my present time…"

"…the two, inseparable, forever…"

"…It's unhealthy, self-harming…"

When Lola finished speaking, nothing remained but a promised resolution, the air between them punctuated by the heart monitor's tempo reading sixty, set to rise regardless of her younger self's would-be words of defiance. The girl cried silently, chest fluttering. The bed mattress warped when Lola settled next to her. She embraced her, kissing her cheek, her forehead, and then allowed her to fall asleep as tears wetted the pillow.

Idle thoughts were dedicated towards inaction alone, because so many words waited in Lola's mind, untold. Perhaps one couldn't explain enough. She'd filled her head with confessions most would never admit, lying beneath intangible thought. This wasn't over.

A flicker.

A pulse.

Her weight gradually disappeared from the blankets. One passenger was left, and soon, only one would ever remain.

Oneironaut

"All dreams end eventually."

- Nev speaking to Heron

For days thereafter, Kronitare's tonic ebbed the mindscape Sweven had leaked into reality; a slow, mythic force dismantling its towers and domes, and its deluge strewn all across the world. Everything receded, but nothing disappeared completely. Crystals snowed on the imaginary structures as a few crumbled and collapsed. And so, a graveyard of architecture remained, watched by silver skies, remembered solely by the one who fed it, who allowed it to prosper, like a plague.

By the journey's end, Lola had developed narcolepsy, a weakened immune system, chronic fever, fatigue, insomnia, and post-traumatic stress. Astrid explained her condition in perhaps greater length than necessary. The maiden was kind, however, fetching up meals and medicine while she lay bedridden. Lola didn't leave her room except to bathe or use the bathroom, as per instructed. Walking any surmountable distance merely provoked her dizziness. Her guard was down—finally—and these symptoms took every advantage.

Breathe, breathe, breathe…

But as the girl's sickness waned, so did Lola's. Soon, she didn't need much aid up the pillar stair flights, nor did she require help in crossing its halls. Stalactite Cove's wonder bloomed now with faded vertigo and fatigue reduced to manageable proportions.

And sleep.

Sleep came like bliss running through her body. She rested twelve hours, twice, covers pulled about her as if to hibernate the season. Raven's silk splayed over pillows and bed sheets as limbs stretched leisurely across the covers. Tinman Tom's schedule had been cleared. Morning roused her instead, like being drawn slowly from aether seas, hypnotically refreshed.

"Your sleep clock's already back to normal," said Yercy. "We've woken up together twice now. Guess we're both morning birds."

Lola nodded, stretching. "My younger half should be able to play our song sooner than later or use the recording device."

"How do you think she's taking it?" After hearing no reply, Yercy sat beside her and asked, "How are *you* taking it?"

She framed the window in a purlicue. "Nothing's healed completely. My fatigue and vertigo remain, somewhat…Sweven too."

"You know that's not what I mean."

Her hand lowered. "Believe me, I know."

They were silent now, watching the light grow brighter outside. Lola's head couched on the nereid's shoulder.

"And there's no use praising my choice, really. Matters plummeted so much before I made it."

"Perhaps the feeling's mutual, then. I'd some wrong assumptions about you, things that would've been better unsaid."

Lola chuckled nervously, then embraced Yercy with all the energy and emotion needed to lighten their words, no pretense necessary.

The nereid slouched back. "But things aren't quite settled yet, are they?"

"Not until the curse breaks, no."

"Shall we leave then?"

Lola slouched too, smiling. "Now there's an idea."

Astrid's welcoming gifts could buy months' worth of food even if one shopped frivolously, which explained Lola's surprise when the maiden let her keep them as tributes to their performance.

"Surely there's been a mistake!" she said. "Free jewelry?"

"The diamonds specifically should pay for your trip back home," Astrid replied. "My nights get pretty lonesome this time of year, so it's been my pleasure. Never forget that you'll always be welcomed back so long as I'm around. Consider us friends."

"Thank you. Thank you so much."

Lola accepted Pearl's offer to finally get her hair cut. Sillstone had been a welcome sight after crossing the prairie fields again, endless gold replaced with tapestries of willows and green spread among the cabins. She nearly dozed off as her locks fell to Pearl's shears until what was left reached just past her shoulders.

Pearl smiled. "Hey, I didn't know your hair would fluff at the ends."

"Me neither." Lola studied the mirror, while Yercy stared in awe.

Honeydew Cape was next. Their wave gliders worked impeccably once the hulls were cleaned of sand delivered by all the previous tides. They trekked across Strevenfall's ocean of glass, of coral reefs akin to aquatic murals strewn for days until the isles appeared and Fervine greeted them with a breeze brushing their clothes.

Brushing Lola, who now visited her parents' old house again, salty brine caked over the wood rotting away to nature. She felt strange, distantly reminded of when torture loomed on every waking day, escape offered only by the night. She stopped amid the rooms that had threatened her so many years prior and played notes touching across old furniture and floors while her mind touched elsewhere, or tried too, at least, recalling times spent playing in houses much like this one.

Another house, abandoned.

Downstairs, she tore off a doll's head to find it bloodless.

Outside, she climbed up the lighthouse, and upon finding a glass shard, flicked it over the rail.

Another house, but different. Yercy's living room steadied her with its ambiance. They arrived here by morning's softest hour before the heat of day had truly come.

"Your home feels like it did months ago."

Yercy grinned. "I believe that's on purpose."

Lola commented during breakfast, "Garenham never felt like home, really, just somewhere I'd live to avoid where I lived before. Guess that choice came from bitterness, too."

"Please...what's the good in deprecating yourself now?"

"No, I still need help, but I know I can still be happy." Lola paused. "Perhaps I'll never get over what they did. Memory is a fickle thing, right? And my own imagination seems to run amok whenever the past gets involved. Who knows if this whole ordeal had a reason for happening. 'Hummingbird's Verse' could be alive for all we've been through together, but there will always be reasons for happiness when all else seems reasonless. I'm never without ways to surmount things no matter how bad they are." She laughed nervously. "Who even says crap like this? Because I just did and it felt amazing, but it's so, so corny. Do I sound corny? I could keep going, though. Let it out, as people say."

"Oh, well, no complaints here", said Yercy. "What better time than now?"

Lola's face warmed.

Yercy asked a different question now. "When do we leave for Garenham?"

But Lola hung on to what the nereid said before, smiling. "What better time than now?"

The train whistled off. Boardwalks curved through the cityscape buildings and pubs, people everywhere, signs directing traffic across noisy roads painted with sunlight. Birds nestled on lampposts, chirping among themselves if not eyeing those with food. Yercy had seldom been to the realm's metropolis. Her eyes marveled as she looked up towards the latticework of steel glistening with recent rainfall.

"Garenham's usually not this crowded," said Lola. "I keep forgetting that summer brings in the tourists, mostly sightseers, but the archives don't flock much attention anyway. Shouldn't be a long wait once we get there."

Bouts of vertigo had her stopping at the parkway benches every now and then. The symptoms warranted nothing else, however, their presence dull and distant. Scattered white buildings marked Sweven's remains— crumbled spires, domes caved in. She found admiration for the dreamworld now, at seeing one's mind meld with reality, an odd reverence that resonated through time.

Time, she thought, *is all I need.*

They didn't travel by carriage no matter how much sense it would've made, for there was no rush, finally. Lola leaned a bit on Yercy. Yercy leaned a bit on her. Passersby moved around them. Droplets littered the sidewalk, shining against the sunlight peeking through the rain clouds

The archive building's design was modest compared to most on campus, like an elder whose name required no distinction. It was such that all who attended class here could study without being interrupted by tourists. The priceless items stored within could bring out the meddlesome side of people, namely thieves.

Shelves longer than the eye could reach, burgundy carpet wedged between them.

Fifty-two floors twined with corkscrew stairs, calm, quiet, compressed.

Cool, dry air vented through the air ducts, vital for preservation.

Gloves and fumigated clothes waited outside the shower room where everyone bathed beforehand, as per required in efforts to minimize contamination. Only then could one search the aisles of songs and documents, some dated several generations back, preserved indefinitely. Elven guards watched with silent eyes. More than half the relics here were valued more than diamonds. The air chilled Lola's skin to gooseflesh.

Yercy hugged her from behind. "You're cold."

"Good thing scrubs aren't the height of fashion, right?" Lola said. "'Hummingbird's Verse' should be here, somewhere."

They searched for hours. Yercy redeemed her lacking knowledge with aid whenever Lola's symptoms returned. She watched her hands comb nimbly through the drawers, through papers old as history, and imagined how life would have been here. Garenham flowed with people, roads filled by day, empty at night. Yercy could well imagine Lola fixed near a lamppost before sunrise, waiting for the carriage as cold rain drizzled down her umbrella, dressed in blue, going about the world with awe towards everything hushed and peaceful. She imagined her attending class to admire the music she played despite her memory's quarrel, a time traveler whose motivation was simple yet infinitely valuable.

Lola's breath caught, a thin binder carefully opened in her palms as if it would snap in two, her mouth on the verge of speaking however speechless.

The first page's title read, "Hummingbird's Verse" in stylized cursive.

The subheading read, *Lyrical rendition.*

Yercy knelt beside her, noticing words printed below the staff lines. "You found it?"

Lola didn't answer, forgetting to move, presently aware yet caught up in another world. She read slowly. Subtle eye movement: her focus carried from page to page—faint flashes of thought, of matters resolving. "I found it," she said, thumb resting at the final verse. "Flowery metaphors aside, the prose hints at a simple cure. Unbelievable, after all this time…"

Yercy caught her eyes glistening. "Hey, no one could blame you for—"

"Crying? N-no." She wiped her face. "I've done enough crying already. Everything makes sense now, yet part of me still hoped the timelines wouldn't need to separate, that I could have it both ways. One might say I'm deranged, demented."

"Again, who could blame you?"

"Enabling me much?" she accused playfully, then her tone softened. "The curse breaks how it began."

"Meaning what?"

"Well, it turns out my ordeal started when I played 'Hummingbird's Verse' months ago, during a night session atop the hills just outside of Garenham. My younger self and I coincidentally played 'Hummingbird's verse' at the exact same moment from different timelines. Performing it together note for note activated the curse, and we inherited time traveling powers as a result." Lola paused. "To reverse it, we must perform the song simultaneously, again."

Yercy leaned in. "And then your syndromes will peter out?"

"Apparently," she nodded, turning to the last page. It seemed blank at first, until a faded signature caught her attention near the bottom, then her eyes widened with recognition and horror.

"What's wrong?"

The binder closed. "Nothing, really. Now I wait to be called back in time again whenever my child half gets well. Guess that leaves us, well, time."

"A luxury, isn't it?"

"Perhaps. Who's to know?"

They spent the week in Lola's apartment—once she'd rented it back from the town—waiting. Just one of Astrid's gem shards could fund several months' worth of payment. They walked Garenham's streets at dawn until night settled and people left, leaving calm in their wake, moonlit curbs dotted with lampposts, vacant lots, whispers carried on the warm breeze. The morning reached over buildings and pools made by thought, over the crumbled bodies of spires slowly falling apart. The dreamworld's architecture wouldn't die completely—at least not yet.

During that week, Lola found what could have been Sweven's greatest anomaly thus far, a great dais ringed by megalithic stones and obelisks, streams flowing around them, and beautiful designs were drawn across the arches bent overhead, some with drapery hemmed across their lengths.

While she was exploring the abstract scenery, a shape caught her attention. It was a statue—a statue of her made from ivory, naked, posed with a calm demeanor despite lacking such modesty. After regarding the plaque at its base, her eyes carefully followed to where it gazed, but she found nothing.

Morningtide surfaced.

A street curb flushed with the day's early glow.

The mattress covers moved. Lola was getting off the bed as a familiar vertigo greeted her.

Yercy nodded. "You know what to say. I'll be here while you're gone."

The hospital's garden teemed with moisture and light hazing through the fog about them, a bright but ghostly white veil. A pool fountain sang as birdlife talked among themselves. Time was moving.

Lola might have been wrong, though, about the movement of time, having brought the girl outside to give her the news on how they would part. Now she waited for her reaction, but there was nothing but stillness. Nothing could have been worse. She gently clasped the girl's forearms. "I'm unsure how to put things in better words. We can't make things better until our song's played concurrently, just like before. And you know my...personal conflict. Helping you wouldn't help much, because I need help too."

Again, nothing but stillness. A slow breath, barely audible through the girl's mouth as it trailed like something lost, emptied, her eyes fixed where sunshine bleached the footpath.

"There's no future in us together," Lola finished, realizing that the girl's manner echoed that of when Valery had punished her, waiting for the doll room's laughter, the confinement, the humiliation. "Please...say something, anything."

And the girl did. "I'm seeing lots and lots of dream stuff too, you know. Lots and lots of pools and junk, just like you said, but I don't mind. I don't mind if you'd just be here and not help me. Being here is enough, really."

I'm not meant to like this, Lola thought.

"Ma and Da will hurt me."

"We're not meant to *like* this, but we *have* to separate."

The girl hugged Tinman Tom closer, turning away, then she was schlepping towards the garden exit with no more to say. Lola followed her until they reached the hospital's recovery branch. The beds here didn't have walls, and her own bed had yet to receive new visitors.

Small hands moved across the blanket, unbandaged, palms clean of injuries.

Lola's hands moved to feel them, regarding her child self, fondly.

"Please don't leave." *Stay until you die.*

"I must leave." *I can't stay forever.*

Lola had said they would perform "Hummingbird's Verse" midday tomorrow, but she knew the girl was thinking to sabotage their plans. She also knew that placing half the burden on her was cruel. However, the desired outcome required consent from both parties. It was cruel for everyone. She'd thought about what to say if things grew quiet, but now, noticing how her words stumbled, realized that the effort had been in vain. This was a separation weighed on themselves, and it was unbearable.

"Here, I made something for you." Lola produced a booklet.

The girl blinked. "Our…dream journal? It looks so different."

"I've written all my notes again where you could read them better. I've also written about my journey through Strevenfall, about you, Pearl, Astrid, everyone—everything I could think of. Our time together reads like a story book, but we know it's true." Lola paused. "These last few months have been something of a dream indeed. Lighthearted. Horrifying. Bizarre. And still I've so much healing left. I'm still quite the chore. Most importantly though, I'm sorry for breaking our promise."

The girl sat there awhile, then brought her head to rest on Lola's lap.

Lola couldn't help but smile. "It's alright. Alright?"

"So, you're actually leaving? No lies?"

"No lies, but in a way, I'll never leave you."

Outside, a tower fell beneath the sun whose glare doused its ivory carcass, and whose rays cut through the mist of morning. Lagoons spilled like a fluvial orenda over the streets where people roamed but didn't notice their feet becoming submerged. A spire cracked. Birds flew among the buildings. Movement strode through the hospital's entry, pastel hair with eyes of watercolor.

Lola nodded to the entry. "And you'll always have someone close."

"Here you are!" Little Yercy rushed to the bedside and climbed aboard, kicking off her sandals. Brimothy watched them connect, witnessing their expressions of glee harmonized through laughter. The girl showed her hands. The nereid touched them.

"All healed?" Yercy chimed.

"All healed," the girl said, before telling her about her older self's departure. She went on simply, without fear or sadness. Yercy moved like how one might comfort another who'd lost something dear. Space and time were all that was left, and Lola felt bittersweet, to watch over their dreams and keep them from falling into the dark. She'd be present for the future when tomorrow faded away. She'd wake to find her past behind her, where it belonged.

The girl smiled faintly.

Yercy followed. "Do you know if things get better?"

"I think so. When we grow up more, I think it'll be okay."

And that's when Lola knew her counterpart was willing to separate, ready for an end. Yercy left. They both rested on the bed, looking up, shoulders touching as clouds rolled above the skylight window. People walked by; ashen cloaks and clothes of every other hue blurred against their peripheral vision.

The girl moved. "She always cheers me up."

"Who, Yercy?" Lola asked, but didn't need an answer. "She'll grow to love you, as I love her now."

"I can't imagine you and me not being together anymore."

"It'll be like a lucid vision, perhaps. Life can feel strange that way."

They lay there companionably, their eyes set adrift towards the atmosphere. They were pilgrims, astronomers through the cosmos, watching Sweven deteriorate as water only they could see poured across the floor. They were idle on the ivory sheets until Lola's body flickered, faded, and was gone, her weight now absent from the blankets.

Alone, the girl climbed out of bed and stepped before a window overlooking the dreamworld's scenery as it crumbled. Those same clouds roamed like sentinels of long-buried astrology. A tower crashed down. A dome caved in. No one but her noticed. Things would be normal again, yet nothing would be the same.

Her thoughts reached out. *Farewell soon.*

Her hands clung to the journal, thankful, afraid.

"Welcome back," said Yercy. "You're still playing the song tomorrow?"

Lola nodded, gazing out the window. "Exactly how it began."

A calm passed over them—a woolgathered era at its end.

Solar Dance

"The elven league has long since been partnered with Typhame. Kain saw Ambright as a unified series of interlocking worlds, 'a cosmic system', as Meisu puts it."

— Cyrus; Typhame's realm guardian

Lola stood still, an early afternoon's whisper touching her hair like a friend and rippling her sundress like magic, the hair as dark as crow feathers, the sundress tiger orange. Smooth rolling hills elevated her a bit closer towards the sun's embrace, and the grass around her swayed effortlessly, waiting patiently. The bright warm scenery welcomed those visiting to observe the clouds drift across the sky. Lola knew this place was more than a simple venue, however, but a stage, one set to come alive with motion.

Her feet rustled along the ground, her heart thumping as she watched the surrounding butterflies and birds rise from their homes around her. They took notice of the woman standing fearlessly atop the hill face and, to a more profound extent, the violin cradled in her hands. She held it like one might a newborn child, and for a moment everything felt like a dream set upon a sunlit stratum, an ethereal plane where all seemed magnificent, flowing, drenched with bittersweet memories. But these days were common during the warm months of Strevenfall, a realm where enchantment like this could thrive and prosper.

The fauna continued watching as Lola raised her instrument and bow, setting them into a fine sturdy posture, an encore held within the form of her limbs. Her feet parted slightly, displacing their weight as to hold perfect balance, ready to spin and whirl about once the notes sped up. She placed her bow across the four silver threads and recalled her previous practice rounds on this same hill, pondering each step until they merged like a subconscious reel playing back in her mind. These snapshots of the past ran between her thoughts, movements she knew by heart, sequences written throughout her mind.

Be still.

Be ready.

It was time to end things.

Lola began. Her bow slid along the wires for a high note wavering free about the air, her eyes closed, her head bowed against the chinrest. She flew confidently amid the upper octaves of sounds as she wove them together, then down a little, then up, her mouth stretching in satisfaction, playing the next adagio as if it were a language spoken by an expert. These were good melodies to start, fine for a short stay, but that was all. Now the bow angled and quickened to produce a snappy plethora of mid keys, and she moved with the tempo, her dress moving in long swells of silk. Louder she went, steadily, boldly, giving each new sound space to breathe before the next one resonated, at times picking off the ends of notes to make a few staccatos. She breached new volume and held it flawlessly, the decibel clean and rich. There was a world to explore here, this myriad of notes ranging from flat to sharp. The brightened tones embellished their shapes, some retaining their separation while others spoke with smooth transitions. Her pace jolted slightly, turning the previously slow tempo into one of agile harmonies. Wind blew as if approving this new, changed rhythm, warm, refreshing, and brushing past her clothes, her hair.

A hot stab twinged her body. It was embraced.

Lola breathed, stopping to rest and regard the smooth landscape of hills watched by the daylight. Another breeze slid across the hill, a welcome presence that excited the fire of her dress, shifting the fabric, maybe brushing off some dust. A far-off crowd might have mistaken her for a wayward spirit, a figure draped in orange. She relaxed as the reel continued in her mind, the next step, the next sound, the future image of her dancing about with every second staged according to plan, without friction between one move and the next. She had become more proficient at playing this song and had forgiven herself for how she once treated past mistakes. The transgressors of her past deserved no such forgiveness, meanwhile; they were not even worthy of attention. Ghosts would always be ghosts, no more a threat to her than her own perception of them.

Her focus clung to the strings as she raised her violin again. One step at a time. First, picture the path, then walk its face.

The performance resumed. The octaves combined as she granted her bow freedom to slant at its leisure, giving leeway into new formations more complex than before, new chords with bolder progressions. She could hop between these levels, pitching her tones, growing louder, more distinct, maturing its density. The butterflies stirred as they watched Lola stray from her spot and move about. Her feet glided across the grass as if in the arms of an invisible partner—dancing with learned precision, making sure not to step on her toes, or trip—a waltz conscious of every sound. She let loose a trill of characters sewn together with smooth legato intervals, climbing up the scale then wrapping around with more intricate patterns. And just when it seemed like the phase would end, she jumped off the ledger line and performed a high presto of short, brisk accents to tie up the chord with emphasis. She whirled about. There were no clear spaces between her movements as she played faster, utilizing the full capabilities of her instrument. She remembered what playing on this hill meant prior to her voyage across the realm, the pain, and her struggle to escape it, to escape her thoughts in fear of what might happen if she embraced reality. While the pain of what happened years and years ago still accented her mind, never to go away, she existed for the here and now, a time traveler valuing this moment and the next above those already long gone.

Another stab.

Burning.

Expected.

And this time a knotted pain curled in her stomach, but she finished the song regardless, proceeding through its last refrain before concluding the session with an easy, fading whole note that flowed off her strings like a breath of fresh air. Only then did she kneel on the grass, letting the pain proceed through her body with knowing readiness. Like an old friend, it was captivating, seeing that phantom image go on playing without her, dancing happily until it vanished with a smile, but there was nothing to be done now, for it was over. One misstep would leave the crowd disappointed even if all else was played perfectly, only this time, there were no missteps, for everything had been planned.

"By the stars," she muttered, "another daunting play."

After a short pause, Lola rose, feeling her spirits lighter—cloaked in the verve of something lost, but also, something more precious gained.

It was a long way back home. She strolled along the narrow sidewalk winding towards her small subdivision, passing an Aezial sanctuary made of domed marble with enormous pillars, around which the expansive grass meadows were broken only by smooth stone gazebos. Even those of prestigious taste would have at least stopped to admire parts of it, but Lola's stare was set towards the horizon where she'd traveled beyond, beyond the oceans and towns and valleys of the world. She got bearings on the sun's position and laughed. Time had elapsed quicker than expected, and it made her finally notice a certain weightlessness crowned on her eyelids, realizing how awake she was, how energized she felt. It was understandable. Playing for a resolution had likely cured the weakness in her bones, with her arms holding the violin secure, not letting go. Perhaps if she walked with more assertion, something marvelous would happen. Then, there she would be, bathed in the folds of daytime with nothing to fear. Nature picked through the silence that had surrounded her before, so her thoughts were free to welcome them, and the future, forever.

It was when the first streetlamp rose into view that Lola knew she was close, its vacant bulb reminding her of a certain someone's imagination, of bulbs like this one coming to life with magic water.

She turned the corner leading to a wider road.

Apartment complexes looked down from either side, with a scent of freshness wafting up her nose, a peculiar feeling, a force of finality, and of new beginnings. It was a nice residence, each structure bound together with curved, complex designs with picket fences and well-trimmed gardens encircling her own apartment, which was four buildings down from the subdivision's entry. Lola's abode sat on the second floor where it had been waiting, but not too long.

Up the stairs, a corner turned, walk several feet, and stop. Lola pulled a key from one of her flats. She leaned against the heavy door with strength not felt in months, perhaps years, her wellness restored and her thoughts clearer than ever. Once the door closed, Yercy went up to embrace her, and she returned the gesture, relieved at last.

"I almost couldn't do it," Lola whispered. "I feel a part of me has died."

The nereid smiled. "It's a part of you that's ready for something greater."

"I love you."

"Likewise, and then some."

They sat at the table and relaxed, remembering, afternoon's aura filtering past the windows with orange and yellow and marigold softening their time together. They would part soon. Lola planned to finish her enrollment at Garenham while Yercy planned to build sailboats at Fervine. But for now, nothing mattered except the moment's serenity. Their bed sheets were in disarray and card games were strewn across the floor. A gramophone played music nearby. It was something called rock, carried over from realms like Vemut and Droodpike.

"I'll be heading back to Fervine come semester's end," said Lola. "I just got my readmission letter signed by Mr. Krayble. He's been a huge help, honesty, along with Axel, and Iris too, handing back my job even after being away this long."

"Four months with change," said Yercy. "But who's counting?"

"Classes start next week, as if what all happened never did, but something did…I got a haircut."

"Among other things! One might think Lola Pern enjoys belittling herself, but thankfully some of us actually know you're the best violinist out there. Alright? Alright then, and that goes for everything else you play. Piano. Flute. There's probably like…ten other instruments. No other student or anyone else even compares, not even close."

Lola couldn't stop grinning. She was mesmerized.

They walked each other down to Garenham's train station where whistles howled, and birds flew over the heads of people passing by. Colored leaves speckled the ground. Steam puffs ambled through the sky rails, towards open landscape, and towards the coast where Yercy's own house waited.

Yercy readied to board.

"I'll send letters from now on." Lola offered half her remaining gem shards. "Here. For good luck, I guess."

But the nereid closed her hand, gently, and said to keep them, smiling all the while. And soon she was waving out her window as the train delivered its parting cry, as it carried down the exit track, down towards Strevenfall's horizon of gold-crested yellow, crowned with orange, metal sounds reduced to a fine echo in Lola's mind.

Lola readied to head back.

I'll definitely send more letters, she thought.

At the apartment, squares of ivory watched her from across the bedroom, a stand holding an open booklet of sheet music. A window above poured rays over the paper consumed with notes and lines. "Hummingbird's Verse" was scripted in large cursive font near the top, and below, a myriad of symbols contained within their rails peered back at her, an audience of ink in all shapes and sizes. This song was flying off her strings hours ago, eight and a half pages of dynamic chords connected with slur lines, rests, repeats, and all manner of markings constructing the extensive piece. She'd heard that no one could ever sing "Hummingbird's Verse" completely, not a human, merfolk, elf, or anyone, suggesting that only an instrument played by hand could explore the music in full. It was also why she knew the lyrics were discarded a long time ago and the song was orchestrated into a purely wordless creation. She remembered holding a version of the song with words strung below its notes, a memory so recent that she could feel its texture. She turned the first page, fingers touching along its surface, exposing another layer of sounds kept in parchment, passing a line where the tempo and pitch climaxed, bringing forth a crescendo, one of the more emotional parts. Past that was a short rest, then a set of eighth notes played in glissando, meaning to slide between them. All of it was rather easy compared to other sections, or even other works of music at this difficulty level, though it still appeared like a forest of ink. However, she knew harder portions waited underneath a few more layers.

Page four came along, a jumbled mayhem of keys and symbols latticed together. And here it was, the measure where one had to jump around the sharp scale with a tremolo, performed by rapidly moving the bow back and forth against a string to create a wavering effect that produced slightly different pitches than normal, prominent overtones. This spot was where her mind had faltered, but no more.

Lola held the booklet between tightened fingers, then tore the pages to shreds, tossing the pieces in the wastebasket, hurting, yet knowingly aware of what lay behind. If she was a beaten child of best intentions, a doubting voice of discontent, a shameful part of one's fruition, at least the future was there, always within reach.

She did, after all, attend one of Strevenfall's most esteemed universities, known for specializing in the advanced musical domain, and that said plenty coming from a realm where the arts already had a firm hold on society. Thankfully, she would soon return there and continue her lessons with Mr. Krayble. He was a wise teacher who taught many, only to befriend a few. Krayble normally welcomed those who wanted tutoring regardless of the hour. Perhaps they would recoup lost times.

Because now, it looked as though time was with her.

The end.

Joseph Gibson is a Palmetto State native and life-long adventurer. One usually finds him either hiking through the foothills of Spartanburg or tinkering with computers closer to the beach.

Printed in the USA
CPSIA information can be obtained
at www.ICGtesting.com
CBHW011812051124
16956CB00038B/563

9 781958 901953